ALWAYS FOREVER MAYBE

ALWAYS FOREVER MAYBE

ANICA MROSE RISSI

HarperTeen is an imprint of HarperCollins Publishers.

For information address HarperCollins Children's Books,
a division of HarperCollins Publishers, 195 Broadway, New York, NY 10007.
www.epicreads.com

Library of Congress Cataloging-in-Publication Data

Names: Rissi, Anica Mrose, author.
Title: Always forever maybe / Anica Mrose Rissi.
Description: First edition. | New York, NY : HarperTeen, an imprint of
HarperCollinsPublishers, [2018] | Summary: High school senior Bee falls in love
with Aiden, who seems perfect for her until his possessiveness leads to abuse.
Identifiers: LCCN 2017034536 | ISBN 9780062685285 (hardcover)
Subjects: | CYAC: Dating (Social customs)—Fiction. | High schools—Fiction.
| Schools—Fiction. | Best friends—Fiction. | Friendship—Fiction. | Abused
women—Fiction.
Classification: LCC PZ7.R5265 Aj 2018 | DDC [Fic]—dc23 LC record available at
https://lccn.loc.gov/2017034536

Typography by Ray Shappell
18 19 20 21 22 PC/LSCH 10 9 8 7 6 5 4 3 2 1
❖
First Edition

For Jo

ONE

IT WOULD BE EASIER IF HE WERE DEAD.

I hate myself the second the thought enters my brain. Hate myself for thinking it, and hate even more that it's true.

Of course it's not true.

I swallow against the thickness building in my throat as I hitch my bag up on my shoulder and push toward my locker, ignoring the murmurs, ignoring the stares. I don't care what they're saying. I don't care what anyone thinks. I only care that Aiden—

No. I can't even think his name. I have to focus on putting one foot in front of the other, on moving forward and making it through this minute, this hour, this day. Without him.

I blink to keep my eyeballs from exploding under the pressure of the tears I won't let fall. I breathe in and try to force the sound of screeching tires and crashing metal out of my brain. *He's still alive*, I remind myself. *He might wake up. He might forgive me.* It's too many maybes.

"Hey, Betts," someone says. I keep walking. "Bee," she calls again. "That ring you wear—is it from Aiden?"

I stop. Turn. Stare.

Cicily and two of her spirit-squad clones stand in their game-day uniforms of matching skirts and matching smirks, assessing me from head to toe. I don't even know what outfit I pulled on this morning, and I'm certainly not going to look. My fingers fly to the ring on my right hand, shielding it from Cicily's gaze. I can't believe she just asked me that.

I will not give her the satisfaction of watching me disintegrate. "Mm-hmm," I manage.

"Did your parents freak out? Mine would flip," one of the clones says. "You guys seem really cute together, though." She tucks a lock of hair behind one ear and blinks her bovine eyes. It hits me that she's not trying to be cruel.

Oh god, they don't know. How could they not have heard—

"Is he coming again after school today?" Cicily asks. She winks. *Winks.*

I think I might vomit. "No," I say. I somehow don't choke on the word.

The third girl twists her necklace around her finger and smiles. "Where did you even meet him? I need to find me a guy like that." The others laugh and the girl adds, *"Vroom, vroom."* They laugh harder.

I shake her words out of my head. I can't have this conversation. Can't pretend it's okay. Can't pretend he isn't gone. Can't pretend it's not my fault.

I turn around and run.

TWO

I MET HIM IN A CANDY STORE.

It was a Sunday afternoon in February, near the end of my shift at the Sugar Shack. I'd been working since ten and had a killer headache from the secondhand sugar high gnawing my brain from all sides. Only thirteen more minutes until I could clock out, but those minutes were dragging like a school assembly on the dangers of jaywalking and meth. I was so ready to release my hair from its too-tight ponytail, ditch my apron and the stupid *Hey, Sugar* visor Mr. Sugarman (yes, really) made us wear, and head out the door. Not that I was eager to rush home for Sunday dinner with my parents. The whole point of this job, besides cash and next year's tuition, was to buy myself more time away from them.

When the bells on the front door jingled, I didn't look up, just kept wiping the grubby fingerprints and streaks of I-don't-even-want-to-know-what off the ice cream case and left the customer care to Lexa. I actually liked cleaning and she actually liked customers, so our shifts always worked out pretty well.

"Welcome to the Sugar Shack!" she chirped at whoever'd walked in.

"Uh, hi," he said. I sprayed another blast of disinfectant across the glass and took a deep sniff. I didn't care if it was killing my brain cells. The sharp tingle of bleach-y chemicals was a welcome change from the candy dust and ice cream air I'd been inhaling all day. It had been a mistake to drink that second root beer on my break earlier, too. I would have killed for some water, three Advil, and a salt lick. "Do you guys have any of those chewy candy frogs?" the customer asked.

"Oh gosh, I'm so sorry," Lexa said. I knew without having to look that she was putting her hand to her chest to hold back the tide of empathy. Even in a freaking candy shop, Lexa was the sweetest thing around. She was like a human kitten, all tiny, wide-eyed, and adorable. If she weren't my best friend's twin brother's girlfriend, I would have had to hate her. "We usually do but we're all out today. Can I help you find something else? We have gummi sharks, gummi worms, gummi dinosaurs, gummi fish . . . and gummi bears, of course."

"Wow. A whole zoo," the guy said.

Scrub scrub scrub. Working at the Shack was largely thankless, but I did get a weird satisfaction out of cleaning like a maniac. And in a candy-store-slash-ice-cream-shoppe, there were endless sticky, sugar-smeared surfaces to wipe. I spent most of my shift downtimes with a rag in hand. Lexa spent most of hers texting Eric.

"My favorites are the gummi octopi," Lexa offered. "They're tasty and cute, and we have them in three colors."

I gazed at the neon lollipop clock, willing it to tick faster. *Eight minutes.*

"Yeah, no, it has to be frogs. It's my little sister's birthday. She's going through a frog phase."

I peeked at the guy's back. Tall. Leather jacket. Shaggy haircut. Tight jeans. I wondered if he played drums in a band or only wished that he did. "We have gummi geckos," I said. "You could get some of those and bite their tails off."

He turned around. Our eyes met, and the slow, sure smile he gave wrapped itself around my chest, squeezed out the air, stopped my heart, and changed everything I knew about anything. At least, it felt that way, since for a few seconds I somehow neglected to breathe.

The cute boys who came into the Sugar Shack were usually eight, not eighteen, and they stopped being cute the moment they opened their mouths and started whining for their parents to buy them something. This boy's mouth held a different kind of danger. That smile was delicious.

I steadied myself against the countertop as he solemnly shook his head. "She's too smart. I'd never get away with it."

I didn't believe that for a second. He looked like he could get away with anything.

"How about a candy crown?" Lexa said, breaking the spell. "You know, like a 'kiss enough frogs and you'll find your prince' kind of thing?"

His lashes were unfairly long. Winter had pinked his pale cheeks above the stubble on his perfect jaw. I had never seen a boy look so pretty yet rugged. "She's not into kissing. She studies them. She wants to be a frog scientist."

"A herpetologist," I said, letting my dork flag unfurl. It flapped in the breeze of embarrassment.

But Drummer Boy looked impressed. "Exactly."

"Well, give her time," I said, like some braver, bolder version of myself. "I hear that nerd girls make the best kissers."

He drew back. "She's nine. And my sister."

I tried not to die. "Right. Sorry. I didn't mean—"

"It's okay." That smile again. It was an offer and a challenge, both at once.

He glanced at the name tag pinned to my chest. Despite the ridiculous visor, I was grateful to be in uniform. True, the Sugar Shack apron covered whatever hint of boob might theoretically have been present, but it also made me look like I actually had a waist. And while I had never looked anything but comical in the tops, scarves, or skirts I'd tried on where there was some kind of ruffle involved, somehow the flounce at the hem of this thing just worked on me. It may have been the most flattering piece of clothing I'd worn, and it leveled the playing field at least a little by flattening out Lexa's amazing rack. The apron was the great equalizer. Also, I liked the pockets.

"So, Joanna—"

"Bee, actually. Or Betts." He arched an eyebrow and I nearly growled with envy. I'd always wished one of my eyebrows could do that. "It's a long story," I said.

"Bee." He considered that with a head tilt. "I like it. It fits. It's kind of . . . cute but sharp. Like a cupcake with thorns."

A shot of pride rushed through me at the weird sort-of compliment. Normally I would bristle at someone I just met acting like he had me all figured out, but this guy—I felt like whatever he wanted me to be, I'd be it.

No. Whatever he wanted me to be, that's what I already was.

It was my turn to speak, but I pressed my lips shut. If I allowed them to open, I might blurt some awful truth like, *This feeling reminds me of Ferris wheels* or *I could stare at your face until sunrise.* Our fizz-and-snap, Pop Rocks connection was making me loopy. Silence was far safer.

His mouth twitched in the pause. "I'm Aiden," he said.

"Aiden," I said, trying it out. It felt right. Everything about him felt right. "Nice to meet you."

He held my gaze. "Likewise."

Saying more could be catastrophic. I stared and blinked instead.

He waited. I stared and blinked some more.

"Well, Bee or Betts," he said, pulling on the wool hat he'd been holding, "the frog hunt continues." He looked straight at me. "I'll see you around." It sounded like a promise.

With a quick nod to Lexa, Aiden pushed open the door. "Have a sweet day!" she called after him.

A whoosh of freezing air burst in, and he was gone. I shivered, less from the cold and more from the certainty that everything in my life was about to change. I stood in the space he'd left behind. Endless possibility unrolled at my feet.

Lexa flipped over the sign on the door, so *COME ON IN, SUGAR* was facing us. She didn't seem to notice the world had shifted. "My turn to close up, right?" she said when I still hadn't moved.

I reached back and yanked at the strings of my apron. I needed to call Jo.

THREE

I STOOD IN THE NORTH HALLWAY, UNWRAPPING MILES of scarf from around my neck and stuffing them into my locker with the hat, gloves, coat, sweater, and leg warmers I'd just shed. The school was way overheated, as usual, but outside it was nineteen degrees before windchill. Living here on the Niagara Frontier, you learned to layer. It was an art.

Jo appeared at my side and handed me a baggie. "Kitchen Bitch delivery."

"Mmm, what is it?"

"Oatmeal cookies."

I held them up for inspection.

"No raisins," she said. "What do you think I am?"

I took one out. "You're the best."

"They have pecans, though. Toasted for flavor and chopped up for texture. I might break instead of chop next time."

My mouth was already full. "Whatever you did, they're delicious," I said, one hand at my lips to hold back the crumbs. The cookies were slightly chewy but buttery soft, with a nutty, caramelized aftertaste. One of the 8,400,237 things I was going to miss about Jo next year—was practically already missing in anticipation of being torn apart by college in six months, a near-future that seemed both too imminent and far, far away—was this: her baking. She was truly talented.

"That's why they call me a masterbaker," she said.

I swallowed. "No one masterbakes as vigorously as you do. It's amazing your palms aren't hairier. You'll probably go blind, though."

"Don't worry, that won't stop me from turning up the heat. And beating and churning. Daily," she added.

"Nice." I pulled a cat hair off her shirt and flicked it to the floor.

"Thanks," she said.

I dug my Chem notebook out of my locker, shoved my backpack inside, and slammed the door shut. "Ready?"

Jo turned and nearly tripped over OJ, who was kneeling on the floor by the locker next to mine, with her papers spread everywhere. "Whoops! Sorry," Jo said, stepping on one paper then another as she tried to catch her balance and move out of the way.

"Jerk-off," OJ muttered, followed by something unintelligible. I walked away quickly so she wouldn't see me smiling and decide I was laughing at her. OJ definitely wasn't known for her great sense of humor.

Jo was grinning too. She wiggled her eyebrows beneath her straight black bangs. "Do you want to get floats at the Shack later? In case he drops by?" I shook my head and fed my face a consolation cookie. She was only mirroring my excitement from what I'd told her last night, but the morning after my Aiden encounter, that excitement seemed way overblown. So we'd flirted. So what? That didn't mean anything would happen. If he went to my school, I would already know. There were only about 130 kids in each class, and most of us started here in middle school.

I dodged a crying freshman. "Yeah, no." I wanted to find a way to see him again, but I'd feel pathetic if I were sitting there waiting for him to show—which he wouldn't, so, even worse. "I hate being there when I'm not on shift. I start feeling like I should be cleaning things."

"You always feel like you should be cleaning things." She had a point. "So come over after school. Tell your parents we need to study for history. Mention Eric so they'll say yes." My parents adored Eric. They liked Jo, too, but they were suckers for her twin. And they were right: Eric was a Very Nice Boy.

"We do need to study for history," I said.

"Correct. And I need to tell you about *my* new crush."

"Wait, what? Who?" This was news. Jo's crushes were extremely rare and selective—as opposed to mine, which tended to be frequent but fleeting, cautiously approached, and easily abandoned when no reciprocal interest was shown, which it never was. The primary thing the few guys I'd kissed had in common was they all had crushed on me first. I'd sparked to that interest, to the thrill of being wanted, as much as to the guys themselves. It was one of the million things about my connection with Aiden that felt so completely different: I wanted him as much as I hoped he

11

wanted me. But Jo would never sell herself short the way I had too often done.

She wriggled in her own dramatic pause. "Sydney."

I stopped. "Sydney MacKenna?"

She looked about ready to burst into song and possibly sprout butterfly wings. "Uh-huh."

I touched her sleeve to ground her. "Recently-rumored-to-be-hooking-up-with-Benji-Watts Sydney MacKenna?"

Jo nodded, still beaming. "She's in my math class."

"Whoa." We kept walking. "So you've finally given up on the fox from *Robin Hood*."

She elbowed me in the gut and I tried not to squawk. "Mmm, the foxy fox. Nah, he's still top of the list. It's not like I'm swearing off guys completely. But I was stalking her a little online last night, and I realized I want to put my face in her face. Like, now. I am smitten."

"Cool. So, what's your plan?"

She shrugged. "I'm gonna wing it and see what happens. You're the one who always needs a plan, not me."

I tried not to flinch, but Jo saw it anyway. She pounced, wrapping me into a bear hug in the middle of the hallway. "Stop it," she lectured. "Fuck what Tyson said. And don't take it as a bad thing. You know I love you exactly the way you are."

I squeezed her back, but the memory of my ex-boyfriend accusing me of being "too uptight" and "incapable of spontaneity"—while also admitting he'd been cheating on me all month—still smarted, weeks later. No, it still raked my gut with its toenails, shredded my dignity with its claws, and punctured my heart with its teeth. Luckily Jo was a human tourniquet. And at least I hadn't slept with him.

"The right guy will appreciate all those things about you too," she said. "And maybe you'll find it's easier to be more relaxed in your next relationship because you won't be dating an unreliable, emotionally abusive shithead."

I squirmed out of the hug. "Okay." I wanted to believe it. "But in my defense, I don't have a plan. Right now. About Aiden. I'm trying to just, like, take it as it comes. If it comes." I was also trying to be realistic. The chances of us running into each other again in a city of 260,000 people were, I had to admit, slim. It would probably only happen if he came back to the Shack to find me, and managed to do so on a day when I was working. More likely he would forget about me, or possibly already had.

"I'm sorry I said it that way. You know I want you to help me strategize."

That part I could do. And I liked feeling needed. "Well, first we should find out if it's true she's got a thing with the quarter-back. That seems like crucial information for us to have."

"Right. That's step one. And if it's true, then step two is that I beat him up after school?"

I shook my head. I worried for her about Sydney being both straight and taken, but if she preferred to joke about it, I would follow her lead. "Nope. You challenge him to a duel. It's classier and more romantic. Shows how much you value her. And it's a good excuse to wear a cape."

She wrinkled her nose. "Maybe I could skip the violence and offer her parents a higher dowry. Reverse dowry?"

"It's called a bride price," I said.

She shot me the obligatory *you read too much* look, then jumped. "I'll outbid him for her on eBay! That's the modern way to get the girl."

"It beats throwing rocks at her window."

We stopped outside the door to my homeroom. Jo leaned against a locker. "Seriously, though. Tell me what you think I should do."

"I will," I said. "But we do need more information."

"All I know about her is she's hot and smart and awesome. She uses black felt micro-tip pens, even for math, and doodles in her notebooks constantly. And she went on that date with Jeremy Packer last year where he took her to the zoo and tried to kiss her in front of the monkey cage, but the monkeys started screaming and pelting him with their poop, so he ran off and left her there, and everyone called him Monkey See, Monkey Doo-Doo for like a month. But that tells you more about him than her, I guess."

"Is that even true?" I asked.

Jo shrugged. "Who cares? It's a great story."

"At least it sets the bar for dates pretty low."

The first bell rang and Jo straightened. "That's my cue," she said. "I'll see you later. Don't cry."

That was *my* cue. "I'm not crying. My eyeballs are drooling for more oatmeal cookies."

"Good," she called, walking away. "You'll have some. After school. Text your parents!"

I waved at her back and ducked into class.

FOUR

I DIDN'T HAVE A PLAN BUT I DID MAKE A LIST, TO HELP Monday move faster and keep my expectations in check. It started, *He probably: 1. Has a girlfriend 2. Flirts with everyone 3. Wasn't flirting even, really 4. Was just being nice 5. Sold his soul to get those eyelashes 6. Has forgotten I exist 7. Is way out of my league anyway 8. Would never make a freaking* <u>*list*</u> *9. Couldn't see straight into my heart to find the very core of my existence, no matter how much it felt like he was doing exactly* that. And so on and so forth, until the last bell rang. I tucked the notebook into my bag and tried to forget about him, too.

But another list, the one I wouldn't write down, scrolled in my brain like a news ticker. *He buys cute, thoughtful gifts for his sister. My name sounds so right in his voice. He saw my dorky, awkward side and still liked me. It takes two to light a spark like that.*

"You're pathetic," I told the inside of my locker. Its metal door clanged shut.

I turned and Jo materialized, mid-rant. "Why even become a teacher if you completely hate humans?" she said as we let the tide of people carry us down the main hall, out the front entrance, and into the light of day. "He's sadistic. These tests are designed to be failed. And not so we'll study harder or learn more from them, just so we'll be miserable and tortured and screwed and he can mock us and feel superior." I pulled out a pack of gum and offered a piece to Jo, but she would not be distracted by cool mint. "It's sick. I used to love history. Remember learning about oral traditions and folktales around the world with Ms. Chopra in sixth grade? That was awesome. Why can't we do that again? We're not even memorizing *useful* names and dates, just the most obscure ones he can think of. The most obscure, white, male ones he can think of."

"Well, it is called *his*tory," I said. We turned toward the senior parking lot, where Jo and Eric had left their little blue car, the Wildebeest. I loosened my scarf and didn't bother with the hat—it was at least thirty degrees warmer than when I'd walked into the school building, eight hours before. Like I said: layers. Layers were key.

"They should rename that class the God-Awful History of Everything Not Important. And if I get a D, it shouldn't count."

Like Jo had gotten anything close to a D in her entire life. She could sleep through the test, drool out her answers, and still score a B-plus. But it wasn't my job to point that out. The myth that we both worked equally hard at things was better left unchallenged. "Aren't you the one who lectured me on how I shouldn't care about grades anymore now that we're second-semester seniors?" The sea of students parted and my feet halted of their own accord. "Oh my god."

"What?"

I gripped Jo's arm. "That's him. That's him that's him that's him. Straight ahead. Leather jacket. Perfect face. Don't look."

Jo looked. "With the *motorcycle*?"

I looked too. He was, in fact, leaning against one. I'd missed that. I had also missed the black helmet tucked underneath his arm.

He lifted his chin. Saw me. Smiled.

All of a sudden, it was no longer winter, and a flock of songbirds hatched from my heart and took flight, throwing me completely off guard. Jo pushed me and I walked toward him, feeling the heat of his gaze as I approached. The heart birdies chirped and looped and soared, like we were in a freaking fairy tale—the good kind. I noticed his stubble and wished for the scrape of it.

"Hey, cupcake," he said.

"Hey, frog hunter." This was too completely surreal.

"Want a ride?"

I looked around for something to confirm this was truly happening. My eyes landed on Jo standing a few feet behind me. She wasn't even trying to keep her jaw shut.

I turned back to Aiden. "On that?" I asked, and gestured toward the motorcycle.

"Yeah," he said. "Or I give a mean piggyback ride if you'd prefer."

My brain flashed on a picture of him galloping around the

living room with his nerdy little sister holding on tight. Adorable.

In the next instant, the image shifted, and I saw *my* arms around his shoulders, my face pressing into his neck. His grip firm under my legs, hair falling into his eyes. Both of us laughing and squeezing each other closer. It felt like a premonition, a flash forward into our future. I already knew we were infinite. Inevitable.

Still, I hesitated. It's not that I didn't want to go or was *incapable of spontaneity*, but I grew up in a house with a lot of rules. I wasn't even allowed in a car with anyone who hadn't had a license for six months. I'd never explicitly been told the rule about getting on the back of a motorcycle with a guy I'd just met whose last name, intentions, and driving record I didn't know, but instinct told me I could be grounded well into my forties. Though since my parents hadn't yet thought to make the motorcycle rule, I supposed I wouldn't technically be breaking it. Especially if they didn't find out.

"I don't know," I said. "My mother warned me never to go piggyback riding without wearing a helmet."

Aiden nodded gravely and reached behind him. "Safety first," he said, producing a dark pink helmet with purple glittery flames on the sides. It looked shiny-new. "This one's mine," he said. "You can wear the black one."

He'd brought me a helmet. I wondered if putting it on would stop my brain from doing so many cartwheels.

"Wait, how did you know I go to this school?" I asked, reason catching up to me. He'd been the only thing I could think about for the past twenty-one hours, but that didn't mean we actually knew each other.

"I didn't." He shrugged. "I guess I got lucky." I don't know what my face did in response to that but, seeing it, he added, "Bee. You look exactly like a Franklin Magnet kid. It's stamped all over you."

Whatever that meant. It was funny to hear, since I had never felt like I fully fit in here. I had Jo, and because Jo had Eric, we'd never been outcasts. We had friends. Eric's popular-boy shine lent us only limited glow, but neither of us had ever needed all that much besides each other.

I didn't want Aiden thinking I was like everyone else at this school. I no longer wanted to belong here. I wanted to belong with him.

He held out the helmet.

I glanced around for any teachers, staff, or administrators who might possibly report back to my mom. I didn't see any, but I did spot Tyson, my ex. He was talking to some girls but most definitely watching us—watching me in that distant, uninterested way that said whatever I was up to, he didn't expect much from it. It was exactly the kind of subtle dismissiveness and belittlement I'd put up with for too long in our relationship. But I was done with letting Tyson make me feel unworthy.

That settled it. I shot an apologetic look to Jo, who mouthed *Go!*, and took the pink helmet from Aiden. It was surprisingly heavy.

Pulling the helmet down over my head, I threw my leg over

the back of the bike and slid onto the seat, right behind him. I hesitated only a fraction of a second before moving even closer and putting my arms around his torso, like it was no big deal, like I wrapped my arms around him all the time, like I was some kind of pro at this. Like I was the star of this movie.

I felt everyone in the parking lot watching us as Aiden revved the engine and said, "You got me? Hold on tight." I snuck one last peek at Jo, who stood, grinning, with a sweetly confused Lexa and a frowning Eric now beside her. I leaned into Aiden and, just like that, we left them all behind.

FIVE

WE TOOK OFF DOWN THE STREET AND I FELT INSTANTLY free, and instantly freezing. Cold air and adrenaline blasted through me as we accelerated into the curves. The motorcycle tilted with the slant of the road and I forced myself not to panic. I leaned against Aiden's calm, confident frame and poured my trust right into him. There was no other choice to be made. I'd already decided *yes* to all of it.

Exhilaration flooded my body as I surrendered control, gave in to the moment, and gave up all feeling in my fingers. I understood now why Aiden favored leather. My chunky knit gloves were adorable but insufficient. I didn't care.

Whatever anyone had thought of me before this, they were wrong. I was wrong. Apparently I *was* the kind of girl who would do something wild and impulsive, because look, I was doing it.

Everything about this was worth it.

"Where are we going?" I shouted over the roar of the engine and the rush of the wind. I hadn't told him where I lived—not that he could take me there—and I realized I had no idea where we were headed.

"What?" he shouted back.

"Where are we going?"

"I can't hear you!"

"Never mind." I tightened my arms around his chest and just held on for the ride. I didn't even know this boy, but I knew I would let him take me anywhere.

"You owe me a story." Aiden peeked at me over the lid of his coffee cup. Green. His eyes were green. I wanted to eat them.

"I do?" I asked. We were walking on a path along the waterfront. He'd taken me to the lake. He'd picked me up on his motorcycle and driven me to the lake and bought me a hot beverage to warm my cold hands while we walked beside the water, which sparkled almost golden in the low winter sunlight. It was the most romantic fucking day of my life.

"Yeah, about your name. Why you're Bee or Betts but your name tag says Joanna. You said it's a long story and I want to hear you tell it."

"Oh. Right." I sipped from the cup that was bringing my fingers back to life, and wished it contained something other than coffee. I had been too embarrassed to order chai or hot chocolate after he'd asked for his coffee black, but I should have gotten a mocha, or at least added sugar and cream. I knew black coffee was an acquired taste but I hoped it wouldn't take too many more sips to acquire it. "It's not *that* long a story. My first name's

Joanna and my last name is Betts. But in sixth grade there were three other Joannas in my class, including my best friend, Jo. We all got different nicknames so it wouldn't be too confusing. The girl who kept Joanna actually moved to Minneapolis or Missouri or something, halfway through the year, but by then I was already Bee, Jo was Jo, and the fourth girl, who refused to take a nickname, got stuck with OJ."

"OJ?"

"Other Joanna."

"Ouch," he said.

"Yeah," I confirmed. "She hates it. Especially since a few of the assholes in our class used to follow her around saying stupid stuff like, 'Mmm, extra pulp.' But she's OJ. Even teachers call her that."

"Well, teachers are assholes too."

"Sometimes," I agreed. A gust of wind blew a few unruly hairs into his face and I resisted the urge to tame them. "At home I'm called JoJo, but by junior high I was ready to switch that out for something you might not name your pet monkey."

"Aw, I'd totally name my pet monkey Betts," he said. "Can't you just see it, riding around in a little sidecar attached to my motorcycle? It could wear little monkey goggles and blow a bugle horn."

I smiled. "And if you bought it a monkey wrench, it could fix up the motorcycle whenever you broke down."

He took a swig of his coffee. The errant hair fell back into place. "I don't need any help fixing Ralph. I rebuilt her myself from parts."

"Wow." And here I'd been proud that I knew how to drive a stick shift. "Wait, your bike's name is Ralph? And Ralph is a girl?"

"All motorcycles are female," he said. If I were Jo, I would have jumped all over that, but he didn't say it like a jerk. "A condition of my getting her was that I had to do all the work to restore her myself. I think my dad figured I'd never be able to do it, but when I really want something, I make it happen."

I liked that about him. "And the name?"

"She's named after Ralph S. Mouse—you know, the mouse with the motorcycle in those Beverly Cleary books?"

I nodded even though I hadn't read those. I had been more of a Beezus and Ramona kind of girl.

"The mouse is male, but whatever."

"Um, that's adorable," I informed him.

He looked pleased and a little embarrassed. "My mom read me the whole series when I was, like, seven, and I got completely obsessed with it. We made this awesome paper mouse mask so I could be Ralph for Halloween. Ears, snout, whiskers, the works. I remember I could barely see out the eyeholes, but I swore that I could because I wanted to be allowed to keep it on while I biked around for trick-or-treating. I didn't want to break character."

I couldn't remember my mother ever helping me with a craft project. Whenever I so much as got out a bottle of glue, she warned me to be careful about making a mess, as if I were still three years old. We'd always had store-bought Halloween costumes. "She sounds like a good mom."

His face went still, and for a second I thought he was angry. "She was, before the cancer. She's not around anymore."

"Oh."

"Yeah."

I didn't know what to say to that. We kept walking and the water kept sparkling, and I wondered what it did to a boy to live through something that sad. He'd had to be so much stronger than I would ever be. "How old were you when she got sick?" I said, hoping it was okay to ask. He'd already shared more of himself than Tyson had in almost four months. Ty was his own favorite topic of conversation, of course, but he was too wrapped up in his enormous ego to truly let anyone else inside. He would never reach Aiden's levels of maturity and self-awareness.

"Fourteen. I was pretty messed up about it for a while," Aiden said. "I got mad at the world and kind of lost my shit. Started fights and caused trouble, talked back to teachers over stupid stuff. Got suspended a bunch of times. Failed most of my classes because I didn't do any of the work."

He tipped back his head to sip the last of his coffee and I tried to imagine this sweet, earnest guy throwing fits and random punches. It didn't compute.

He tossed his cup in the trash. "By the time Mom was gone, I'd gotten kicked out of high school. My dad tried to make me enroll somewhere else, but I was done. It all seemed like bullshit and I didn't want to play along with what anyone else thought I should be doing. I just said 'fuck it' to everything."

His voice was intense but the words were so honest and raw, I wanted to wrap him up tight and protect him from all his pain. Yet I didn't quite dare to touch him.

"Sorry," he said. "I don't usually tell people all this stuff." I shook my head. He didn't need to apologize. "There's just something about you that makes me feel like I can trust you with anything."

My blood went effervescent. "You can," I said. I was glad he did. It made me want to prove him right. It made me want to prove myself worthy. "So you . . . built a motorcycle? And got better?"

The smile spread up his face and into his eyes and I no longer needed the coffee for warmth. "Kind of," he said. "That was part of it. Having a project I had to work hard at, and showing myself and everyone else that I could do it—that was huge. And I just finally grew up a little, I think. I realized I'd been lashing out at the wrong people over all the wrong things. Setting a terrible example for my baby brother and sister. Causing all kinds of extra trouble for my dad. None of them deserved that. And I was screwing myself over too. So I pulled it together and got a job and a GED, swore off drinking and all that shitty behavior, and started trying not to be such an ass all the time."

"Is it working?" I teased.

He poked me with his elbow. "You tell me."

"Hmmm." I tried to look critical. "I may not have collected sufficient data to draw a firm conclusion yet."

Aiden took out his keys and I realized we had already looped back to where we'd started. "Then you'll have to let me see you again. We'll conduct further studies. For the sake of science."

"Okay," I agreed. "For science."

We grinned at each other for at least eight extra beats, and for one heart-pounding second I was certain he would kiss me, but he pulled out his phone instead. "Tell me your number?"

He punched in the digits and hit send so I would have his too. I checked my screen to see one missed call from him and seven texts from Jo. It was later than I'd thought. I put the phone away. "I'd better get back before my parents freak out."

"Sure. I'll drop you home." He unlocked the helmets.

I cringed. "Is it too weird to ask you to leave me a few blocks away? I'm not sure they'll be cool with my showing up on the back of a motorcycle."

"You mean you haven't been riding bitch your whole life? You're a natural."

I got serious. "No, and I want to do it right. Teach me how to do it better."

He pulled on his gloves. "I'd say you're doing great."

"Should I, like, lean into the curves, or try to stay upright? Or something else?"

"Betts." He kissed the tip of my nose. "Don't think. Just feel it."

SIX

AS I FLOATED UP THE SIDEWALK TOWARD MY HOUSE, I saw I was in luck: no cars. My parents weren't home yet.

I scrolled through Jo's texts—mostly exclamation points and question marks—let myself in the door, and bent down to greet Rufus, our dog. I tousled his ears while he sniffed my coat and face with suspicion. I loved the idea that he could smell Aiden on me, that our scents had mingled together and now, even after we'd parted, the new perfume of *us* remained on my clothes and skin. That Rufus could smell the caffeine and adrenaline and happiness seeping out my pores.

My phone buzzed. **Are you pregnant yet?** Jo asked.

Almost, I answered. I dumped my bag and headed to the kitchen. **We went to the lake he kissed my nose he is perfect and so pretty and ahhhhhhh**

I washed my hands and filled a tall glass with water as Jo sent a string of dancing emojis in reply.

Rufus ran to the front hall and I heard a car door slam shut in the driveway. **Parents home talk later,** I wrote. My mom walked inside, balancing a pizza box, her purse, two totes, and a pile of papers. I put down my water and went over to help.

"Why haven't you set the table?" she asked as I took the pizza box from her hand.

"Fine, how was your day?" I set the pizza on the counter and pulled open the silverware drawer.

"Don't be fresh." Mom unloaded her bags with a sigh and slipped off her shoes before heading upstairs to change. My brother, Kyle, could have gotten away with a comment like that, but of course coming from me it fell flat. My sense of humor didn't translate with my mother these days. If I were smarter I would just keep my mouth shut.

I filled two more water glasses and carried all three to the table, trying not to hum. Despite my mom's crank, my good mood was hard to suppress, but it might set off parental alarm bells.

Rufus danced at the door again. "Hi, Dad," I called. He dropped his keys into the key dish and grunted in reply.

Three plates, three napkins. I went back to the kitchen for red pepper flakes.

"Did you put out the waters?" Dad said into the fridge, like I didn't set the table, including waters, every single night.

"Yup, got it."

He straightened, opening a beer. "Good." The liquid fizzed and cackled while he split it between two glasses.

I followed him to the dining room and slid into my usual chair. "Open the box, let's eat," Mom said as she walked in, smoothing the hem of her shirt. My mom was a high school English teacher—not at my school, thank goodness—and she spoke to everyone she encountered like they were unruly children it was her job to discipline. Especially me, and especially lately, with whatever was going on with the new head of her department making her come home every evening extra nerved up and exhausted. I'd never have called her a shiny, happy person before, but this school year was making her miserable. Thank goodness I'd had Jo's as an escape hatch.

I blotted the grease from my pizza and folded over the paper towel while my parents complained about their days—Mom grumbling about a memo on expectations for standardized test scores, Dad reporting on the guy at the deli who still couldn't get Dad's order right, no matter how many times he said *no mayo*.

I let their voices recede into nothingness as I replayed the afternoon in my head. I wanted to remember every detail of every second Aiden and I had spent together. Every look he'd given me. Every word he'd said. Each moment our bodies had touched or almost touched. I could see the slow lift of his smile, the way it started with a quirk in one corner of his lips and grew until it reached his eyes. His eyes that were so vivid in my mind, I could almost count the lashes. He was the realest person I'd ever met.

"JoJo."

My head snapped up at the sound of my name. Both my parents were watching me closely. I swallowed the giant bite of pizza I'd been chewing, cheese glomming onto the sides of my throat as it went down. "Hmm?" I managed to say around it.

"I said, how did the studying go?" Mom repeated.

Studying. "Oh," I said. "Great. Fine. It was fine." I reached for my water as an excuse to hold something in front of my face while I lied. Though I sometimes bent or partially evaded their rules in order to make my life more livable, I never straight-out broke them like I had today. Kyle did, all the time, ever since we were kids, but I'd never quite dared. I didn't have that Kyle charm that often helped him get away with it, and I was kind of a goody two-shoes anyway. Yet somehow I was the one our mother always seemed suspicious of. As Jo pointed out, there were endless double standards for girls, including those enforced by other women. "We got a lot done," I elaborated.

I braced myself, certain that once my parents really looked at me they would know. The spark of Aiden's kiss had set off a glow that had radiated across my cheeks, seeped into my skin, and gone coursing through my veins. The change had to be all over my face. How could they not sense it? I expected them to pounce on the lie and demand to know where I'd been.

But for all their careful monitoring, my parents clearly didn't see me. Mom nodded. "That's good. I hope you've still got energy for your other work, though. Surely history isn't the only thing on your plate." One would think, since I'd already gotten into college, she might trust I had it under control. One would think wrong.

"Yeah, I'll probably be studying the rest of the night." I would probably also be texting with Jo, but of course I wasn't going to say that. Even if I hadn't supposedly spent the afternoon at her house, my parents would still want to know what we could possibly need to talk about when we had already seen each other all day at school. My parents did not have real friends of their own, and it showed.

I took another slice of pizza, trying to choose the one with the fewest mushrooms. Mom still got our pizzas with Kyle's favorite toppings even though my brother had been at college for almost a year and a half. Seventeen months of the parental scrutiny focused solely on me. Although if Kyle were here, he would still be the golden child—whereas my parents treated me like I was a toddler playing with knives at the edge of a cliff.

It could be worse. I could have the kind of parents Lexa had—the mom-and-dad versions of Lexa herself, who acted like their kids' own personal cheerleaders or their overaged best friends. I didn't want that. But it would be nice to have parents who fell into some sort of middle ground. Like Jo's parents, who were supportive of her and Eric's lives, but not all up in them, either, because they had lives of their own. But the Metmowlee-Ruben family was basically perfect. It was pointless to compare.

"May I please be excused?" I asked, rolling up my napkin to put back in its ring. I couldn't tell my parents about Aiden yet, but the everything of him was so good, it was hard to contain it. I needed to get upstairs so I could let it all spill out with Jo.

My father eyed my empty plate. "Yes, if you clear your dishes and put away the pizza box."

I jumped up. "We're having ice cream later if you'd like dessert," Mom said.

"No, thanks." My phone buzzed in my pocket. "I already ate a few cookies at Jo's."

I pulled out the phone on my way up the stairs. One new text from Aiden: **Hey**

Hey, I wrote back.

You free on Friday?

I might be

I'm picking you up at 6. Dress warm

SEVEN

"WITH THE SCARF OR WITHOUT?" I ASKED, TURNING away from Jo's mirror to model both options.

"Without," Jo said. "Don't hide the V-neck. You want to show off some skin."

"No, with," Eric said. "He said to dress warmly, right? If he picks her up on that motorcycle, she'll freeze."

"It's not that cold tonight. And she'll be warmed by the heat of his loooooove. Plus a coat."

"Wear it," Eric said to me. "You can always take it off later."

Jo wiggled her shoulders, shaking the queen-size bed where they sat side by side. "She can take it allllll off later." Eric rolled his eyes.

I put the scarf back on. Now that Friday was finally here, my dizzy high from the past few days was swiftly crashing down. Aiden and I had been texting cute banter and funny, random pics all week but I felt nervous and almost shy about seeing him again. The scarf was good armor.

"Maybe you should add *more* layers," Jo said. "I bet it's a fetish. He wants you to wear as much clothing as possible so it takes him hours to undress you."

I shook my head. "Stop. He's not going to undress me. We haven't even kissed yet. And that's not a thing." I didn't want to joke around about this, but of course Jo pushed it further.

"Sure it is! It was a thing for me."

"Oh boy. Here we go," Eric said.

"No, really. It was my first sexual fantasy. When I was eight years old I used to jerk off while picturing my wedding night— which was, of course, the first time I would be doing it. I knew my new husband would be very, very handsome and I knew we'd be in a hotel room and he'd kiss me and we would do stuff on the bed, but I didn't really understand what the stuff *was* or what he might look like naked, so I imagined us both wearing tons of clothing so I could fantasize about removing layer after layer without having to get to the really scary part before I was finished."

I would never even think the words *sexual fantasy* in front of my brother, but Eric and Jo had always been different. He was unperturbed, at least by that part. "You were masturbating when we were *eight*?" he said. "I'm not sure whether to be alarmed or impressed."

Jo shrugged. "Perks of being female. Tell him, Betts."

"Nah, that's okay," Eric said before I could decline to get pulled into it. I hated when she used me as a prop in the Jo Show, even when our audience was Eric. Or maybe especially when our audience was Eric. He stood and wiped his hands down his jeans. "I've gotta go layer up for Lexa now anyway. Have fun, Bumble Bee. See you at breakfast."

I stuck out my tongue in response to the nickname (while behind his back, Jo made a face at the mention of Lexa) and he laughed as he crossed the room. Eric was the only one who could get away with calling me that.

Jo narrowed her eyes at the door he'd shut behind him. "Something is up with him."

"Because he doesn't want to hear about your earliest sexual fantasies? That seems like normal brother behavior to me."

"Hmph." She blew her bangs off her forehead. They fell straight back into her eyes.

She didn't elaborate on her theory about Eric and I didn't push. Jo was my best friend but Eric was her twin, and she was both twin territorial and older-sister protective of him. It could get intense. On their eleventh birthday, Jo's gift to Eric had been a poem she wrote about how she sometimes wanted to kill him but would nonetheless take a bullet for him, eat the poison apple, fall on a knife, drink the cyanide, or accept an arrow through the heart, no hesitations, no regrets, so they could leave this world as they had entered it: together.

He had given her a pudding cup. Butterscotch.

Jo had been writing a lot of dramatic and macabre poetry at the time, but still. I'd learned early it was best not to insert myself anywhere near the middle of that.

For about ten seconds of sophomore year I thought I was in

love with Eric. It was the only real secret I had ever kept from Jo, but falling for your best friend's brother, let alone her twin, crosses all the lines of acceptability. Jo would have taken it as a straight-up betrayal. Eric was *hers*. And I wouldn't ever want her to look at me with the same mix of tolerance and mild disapproval with which I'd seen her eyeing Lexa and the other Lexa-types he'd gone out with before her.

Besides, it was pretty obvious at the time that my crush was in no way requited. Eric loved me, but not in that way. And I wasn't even sure that my feelings for him were really about *him*. It was hard to separate loving Eric from loving the whole package deal—Jo, their parents, this house. Even Stella, their terrible cat. I loved everything about the entire Metmowlee-Ruben household. I always had. *My* childhood fantasy had been that I would wake up one day and be one of them.

But just as I would always be Jo's best friend but never her twin, I would always be welcome in this home but never belong here, no matter how long I stayed or how many of their snacks I consumed. I wasn't a charismatic, talented, extraordinary Metmowlee-Ruben. I was an uptight, control-freakish, self-doubting Betts.

Except maybe with Aiden I could be something else, a different kind of girl. The kind that would climb onto the back of a near-stranger's motorcycle, putting her life and her heart in his hands because he'd asked. There had been a power and a freedom in deciding to give myself over to what fate had thrown my way—to wrapping my arms around him and being fully in for the ride.

I felt safe with him. I felt central, already.

I took off the scarf. "You sure you're okay with my ditching you tonight?"

"Okay with it, yes. Thrilled about it, no," Jo said. "But I know you won't make it a habit."

"Never," I swore. If things went as well as I hoped they would tonight, I'd ask Aiden to take me on a "first" date and meet my parents, and Jo wouldn't have to be my cover anymore.

Jo widened her eyes. "Incoming," she said. I turned toward the window. It was too dark to see out but there was the unmistakable hum of a motorcycle approaching. "Go. I'll see you after. Come back with juicy details, okay?"

I gave her a quick kiss on the cheek. "Okay." I threw on my coat, stuffed the scarf in the pocket, and flew down the stairs, nearly tripping over Stella at the bottom. *"Meowww,"* she complained. I walked right past.

I slipped on my shoes, reached for the doorknob, and took a deep breath.

He was here.

EIGHT

I WALKED DOWN JO'S FRONT STEPS INTO THE COLD OF early night, toward the boy who was waiting for me. Aiden lifted off his helmet and ran a gloved hand through his hair as he watched me approach. His face stayed solemn as I moved toward him, drawn in like he was my gravity.

I stopped one step short of pressing against him. "Hey," I said.

"Hey." He pulled off his gloves and, without breaking eye contact, reached for the zipper of my halfway-fastened coat and zipped it all the way up to my neck. His fingers brushed my chin. "There," he said.

"Thanks."

He held my gaze a beat longer and swept a hand toward Ralph. "Shall we?"

"We shall."

I didn't ask where we were going. I didn't need to know. I pulled on the helmet he held out to me, swung my leg over his bike, and wrapped myself around him. This was where I belonged.

* * *

"You been here before?" Aiden asked as we walked up the road into Cazenovia Park.

"Sure," I said, "but not at night. Are we allowed in here after dark?"

Aiden reached for my hand and we passed through the glow of an old-fashioned streetlamp. "You don't want to go all Bonnie and Clyde with me?"

I pretended to consider it. "I'm not sure I'm dressed for a full-blown crime spree," I said, thrilling at the easy way our arms swung in sync. "I'd consider jaywalking, though. Or illegally downloading something."

He gave my gloved fingers a squeeze. "The park's open until ten. I will not make you an accomplice to my crimes. Not tonight, anyway." He led me off the pavement onto a dirt path along the creek. It was darker here away from the streetlamps, but not as dark as I would have expected. The sky glowed purple-gray from the lights of the city, and there was a nearly full moon sliding in and out of the clouds over the spidery canopy of branches above us. Our footsteps in the gravel and the distant traffic were the only sounds.

We came to a small clearing beside the water and Aiden let go of my hand. He shook out a blanket he'd pulled from his bag and spread it on the dead grass. "I hope you like picnics."

"Everyone likes picnics. But who picnics in winter?"

"We do," he said. *We.* I liked the sound of that. "Sit."

I arranged myself cross-legged on the blanket and shifted on the lumpy, frozen ground beneath my butt. Perhaps this was why only *we* picnicked in winter: Winter was cold. Aiden draped a second blanket across my shoulders and I cuddled into the cozy fleece of it. Much better.

He kneeled and uncapped a thermos. Steam escaped in wisps that curled up toward the moon as he poured me a cup of something hot. I held it to my lips and breathed in the scent. Coffee. Black. Of course.

I took a small sip. Nope, still not used to it.

"Good?" he asked. I nodded and braved another taste. It was bitter, but I appreciated its heat. And even though I didn't like it, I loved the idea of it—of drinking it here with him, in the park at night on a picnic during the first chilly weekend of March.

"Bread. Cheese. Coffee. Chips." Aiden named each item he'd laid out. "And Devil Dogs for dessert."

"Amazing," I said, accepting the hunk of baguette he ripped off the loaf for me. I tore it open with my thumbs and piled a few slices of cheddar inside.

"You warm enough?"

I nodded and chewed, marveling at how much better everything tasted outside. "You?"

"I wouldn't say no to sharing some of that blanket."

I lifted one end and Aiden scooched closer. My butt was numb and it was cold enough to see our breath, but I no longer felt the chill. There was only the buzzing awareness of his body so close to mine. I narrated the cheesy romance-novel version to Jo in my head: *The winter's cold melted away in the fire of her anticipation. His chest heaved with masculine tenderness and her bosom swelled to almost a real B-cup as her lips and loins tingled with the desire for his kiss.* I stuffed more bread and cheese in my face to hide the grin. Elation was making me punchy.

I looked up at the sky. "How's your knowledge of constellations?"

"Pretty weak. Yours?"

I pointed at the blinking lights of an airplane. "I think that's Halley's Comet."

He squinted. "Nah. It's a falling star."

"Oh. Better make a wish, then," I said.

He closed his eyes to play along with the joke and when he opened them, gave me that trademark slow smile. "There you are. My wish come true."

I grinned. It was corny but also perfect. I felt lucky to be with him, too.

He bit into his cheese sandwich and helped himself to the thermos-top of coffee I'd been sipping from before. I turned to watch the creek. I'd lived in this city my entire life but somehow Aiden was showing me whole new sides of it. "It's beautiful here."

He nodded. "I love this spot. There's never anyone here, no matter how crowded the park is. It's like my own secret world no one even knows exists."

"Except me. Now I've invaded."

"You're not invading. I invited you in."

He passed me the coffee and I brought it to my lips, my mouth touching the spot where his had just been. The steam warmed my cheeks and the coffee slid down hot. Maybe I was starting to like it. "So you come here a lot?" I asked.

"All the time. It's a good place to think." He took a handful of chips. "I found it a few years ago while my mom was getting treated over at Mercy Hospital. I was wandering around the park and I just felt drawn here. Kinda like how I was drawn to you."

I couldn't get over how open and sincere he was. I was so used to guys who couched everything they said in posturing and sarcasm, lest anyone mistake them for vulnerable human beings with real emotions inside. I was so used to talking that way myself. But Aiden apparently didn't feel the need to protect himself from me like that. He was so honest and trusting. It made me want to trust him with all of who I was, too.

Probably it came from everything he had gone through with losing his mom so young. It made him so much more intense than anyone else I'd known. "How long was she in treatment?" I asked.

"Two years."

"I can't even imagine."

He grimaced and reached for the thermos. "It was hell. But better than what came after."

He refilled the coffee and I accepted the fresh cup. "I've never been close to anyone who died," I admitted into the steam. "My dad's father passed away before I was born and I still have my other three grandparents."

A funny look crossed his face. "She's not dead," he said. "My mom's still alive. She lives in Arizona."

"She . . . what? I thought . . ." I didn't finish the sentence. It was embarrassingly obvious what I'd thought.

He made a bitter sound that almost resembled a laugh. "Though I guess you could say she's dead to me."

I felt suddenly aware of the cold again.

His shoulders fell. "I know I shouldn't say this out loud, but sometimes I wish the cancer had killed her." He looked down. "It would be easier than knowing she chose to leave."

They were the saddest words I'd ever heard. I didn't know what to say, so I reached out to take his hand. His fingers tightened around mine, and in his grip, I felt the depth of his sorrow and need. When he glanced back up his expression was pained and urgent. "Promise you'll never do that to me."

My pulse skipped with a kick of surprise, and my first instinct was to draw back, but I held steady, though my voice wavered. "I—I promise." Leaving him was the opposite of what I wanted to do, and saying it out loud made that feeling even stronger.

His fingers relaxed and the storm cleared out of his eyes. My heartbeat slowed to a normal rate. If this was a test, I was glad to have passed it. "Good," he said. His face glowed pale in the moonlight but I still saw it flush. "I'm sorry, I don't mean to get weird and scare you off. I just . . . Bee—" He stopped talking and I stopped thinking, for the near-infinite moment before he kissed me. Soft. Sweet. Questioning. His lips pressed to mine for only a few seconds before he pulled back. "Okay?" he asked.

His gaze was serious but I couldn't help the smile that pushed at my cheeks as I nodded. It was more than okay. It was the best first kiss I'd ever had. I missed his lips already. "Yes."

He tugged at the blanket to pull me close, and tucked himself around me.

NINE

I WOKE UP SATURDAY MORNING, ALONE IN JO'S BED, to the scent of something delicious. Whatever Jo was baking us for breakfast, it seemed to involve nutmeg. I stretched out my legs into her side of the bed and looked at the clock: 10:13. Bless Jo's parents for always letting us sleep in, rather than insisting everyone be up before eight like my parents did.

I snuzzled deeper into the pillows and Jo's fluffy comforter and let my body awaken slowly to the blissful reality of him: *Aiden, Aiden, Aiden.* It pulsed through me like a heartbeat. I wondered if he was thinking about me too as he changed people's oil and tightened their gaskets, or whatever it was he did working the early shift at Percy's Garage.

I loved that Aiden had actual skills. Nobody else I knew could do anything useful. Jo could bake fancy treats and Eric could kick a ball into a net and my brother could do the kinds of things philosophy majors did—think?—and I could clean and organize and obsess, but none of that would get us through the zombie apocalypse, unless zombies could be stopped by croissants and Plato's Allegory of the Cave. But Aiden could build and fix things, and his hands were skilled and useful. That was hot.

I touched my chin, feeling the sting of where his stubble had sandpapered it raw as we'd kissed and kissed and kissed in the moonlight. It was probably red. I hoped so. I liked the idea that his kisses had marked me. Jo would be appalled, but it was sexy to me. I added it to the brand-new list of Things I Wouldn't Tell Her.

It had been strange, late last night, to find myself holding back with her. It felt like I was telling Jo everything, yet sharing nothing. There was so much about Aiden and me that couldn't be described or explained. Like how with every kiss I had wanted to freeze time—to hold on to the moment and make it stretch forever, full of the promise of everything we might become. But I'd also wanted to fast-forward—to speed into our future and consume it all in one gulp. I was greedy for us. Eager and stingy and nostalgic, all at once.

Suddenly there were parts of me only Aiden understood ways I just made more sense when I was near him, like I'd been a jumbled Rubik's Cube he solved with one turn, or a puzzle missing the pieces he snapped into place. He saw the sexiest, most daring, best version of who I was, and brought out sides of me I hadn't known were there. And he trusted me with parts of himself I knew no one else saw—how the sadness in his past made him both strong and vulnerable. How his toughness hid layers of anger and pain. That rawness at his center made me want—no, need—to wrap him in a love that would protect him from the entire world. To be, as I had promised, the person who would never hurt him.

Even though usually I was the practical one and Jo was the romantic, I knew she wouldn't get it. To her, Aiden was still some guy I had only just met—a fun rebound to help me fully move on from Tyson. But to me, we were already an *us*. I couldn't explain that to Jo. I didn't want to. Some things can only be felt.

But that didn't mean I couldn't go eat whatever she was baking. I had to get up soon anyway or my bladder was going to explode.

I climbed out of bed, straightened the comforter to make it look neat, and helped myself to Jo's fleecy green robe. As I headed toward the bathroom, I checked my phone.

Good morning ♥

He was too good to be true.

The air in the kitchen was warm and thick with butter and sweetness. I slid onto a stool and watched Jo pull a tray of mini muffins from the oven with pot-holdered hands. "Raspberry chocolate chunk," she said. "And whole wheat, so they're good for you."

"Chocolate is good for me too," I said, and plucked an already cooled one from the basket on the counter.

"Agreed." She released the hot muffins from their tray, lined them up on the cooling rack, and snapped a photo to post. Hundreds of her followers were probably already drooling. Jo was food-blogger famous. I had no doubt her baking would make her real-world famous someday too. She'd already turned it into a brilliant college essay. My two essays—about my love of word games but not spelling bees, and the day we helped my father's mom move into an assisted-living retirement home—were far less impressive or enviable, though apparently they had done the trick. I'd been accepted early decision at SUNY Geneseo, a really good school, but soon Jo would get into a great one. Her parents would pay for the whole thing, too. There were perks to being the daughter of two doctors.

I polished off the muffin in three bites. "These are amazing. Seriously."

Jo beamed. "You think so?"

I grabbed another one. "I want to marry them." I split open the second muffin and shoved half in my mouth. Tart-sweet-chocolatey yum.

Jo's baking obsession had started on a family trip to Paris, where the Metmowlee-Rubens took a private lesson with a real French pastry chef. We were ten, and it seemed like the most exotic and sophisticated thing I had ever heard of anyone doing. Since then she and Eric had ridden horses in Argentina, walked through cloud forests in Costa Rica, and seen golden-roofed temples, giant Buddhas, and wild monkeys while visiting their relatives in Thailand. I had barely left New York State.

"Mmph!" I swallowed. "I know what you should do. You should bake these for Sydney. One taste and she'll be yours forever."

"Stop," Jo said, but she was clearly pleased.

It wasn't a bad idea, though. "The way to a girl's crotch is through her taste buds," I advised.

"You need to pay better attention in anatomy."

"I'm pretty sure that's Shakespeare."

We heard the front door open and close, and Eric walked into the kitchen, red-faced and glowing from his run. He gave a sharp nod. "Hello, beloved sister. Killer Bee."

"Hey." I leaned away as he reached across me to grab a muffin off the rack. He smelled like cold air and cedar deodorant and boyness.

"Please," Jo said, "sweat all over my muffins. Who needs a shower among friends?"

"I'm so glad you feel that way." Eric popped an entire mini muffin into his mouth and reached for a second.

I stood and got a clean mug from the dishwasher. Dr. Ruben had left half a pot of coffee warming in the sleek, curvy machine. Money maybe couldn't buy happiness but it had bought Jo and Eric's parents a really nice kitchen filled with tasteful chrome appliances. There was a many-spouted espresso maker right beside the drip machine, but I didn't know how to use it and didn't need anything that fancy. I poured myself a cup and inhaled the steam. *Aidan.*

Jo stared as I carried the mug to my seat. "Coffee? Black? Who *are* you?"

I shrugged and took a small sip. It was funny she found my coffee drinking outrageous when she'd been all for my getting on a motorcycle. But *she* would have gotten on the motorcycle, for sure. Maybe that was the difference. Jo would not drink her coffee black. "I'm developing a taste for it," I said.

"Since when?"

"Since Monday," I admitted.

"Ah." Jo's lips twisted at the corners, and I wished I didn't feel defensive. But this wasn't about the coffee, it was about me falling in love. That wasn't something to smirk at.

"People were asking about you at the party last night," Eric said with his mouth full.

"Me?" I said.

"Yeah. They wanted to know about you and Motorcycle Man."

"Who wanted to know?" Jo pressed.

"Well, Tyson, for one." I couldn't help feeling triumphant about that. "Cicily. Fatima. Bunch of girls, I dunno."

"What did you tell them?" I asked. I hoped whatever it was had made Ty feel like shit.

Eric shrugged and took what must have been his fourth or fifth muffin. That boy ate more than anyone else I knew and was approximately as wide as my pinkie. "Not much."

"Was Sydney MacKenna there?" Jo asked. I knew instantly from her casual tone and lack of eye contact that she hadn't told Eric about her crush. Which, fair enough. I didn't tell my brother about my crushes either.

"Syd? Yeah, I saw her." I waited for his twintuition to alert him there was something more to this question but, despite whatever superpowers they'd developed in the womb, I still was sometimes better at reading Jo than he was. "Hanging off Benji Watts," he added.

Jo turned toward the sink. She slammed the water on full-force and stuck the muffin tins under it. I stopped feeling slighted and just wished I could hug her.

Eric looked at me. "What happened to your face?"

"What? Oh." I touched my chin. "I scraped it."

He squinted. "On what?"

Jo turned back around. "On her new boyfriend's tonsils."

Eric paused. "Oh." He gestured with his three-hundredth muffin. "I thought maybe you'd hit the pavement. Did you know you're thirty-five times more likely to die on a motorcycle than in a car crash?"

"Me personally?" I asked.

"Well *now*, yeah," he said.

I grinned. It was cute that he'd looked up statistics. I loved it when Eric tried to big-brother me. I loved any reminder that I was part of them. "Did you know that nosy friends are eighty-six percent more likely to get pelted with mini muffins, and forty-three percent more likely to die of a chocolate chunk overdose?"

He laughed and held his hands up, backing away. "Okay, you can take care of yourself. Just don't let your mom ever see you on that thing."

My smile dropped. "I know. She's one hundred percent likely to kill me." Though with luck she would never find out about that part. Aiden had agreed that when he met them, he would pick me up in his father's sedan.

Eric went up the stairs, taking them two at a time, and I wrinkled my nose at Jo. "Sorry about Sydney."

"Yeah." Her nose wrinkled back and her freckles danced. "Bummer."

"At least now we have the info?" I said. But her downplaying the disappointment was worrisome. Jo tended toward the dramatic, so it wasn't a great sign when she acted reserved.

"Right. Success," she said. She dried her hands on a dish towel and tossed it at my head. I swatted it away. "Don't worry, I'm not crying. That's just a sugar crystal on my face."

"Oh, from your not-crying pie," I said, nodding.

"Exactly." But I hated the way her shoulders drooped. I wanted her beaming like in the first-day-of-kindergarten photo on the fridge, where she was clutching Eric's hand and they were both wearing red for good luck, like on every first day of school since.

"You wanna cuddle and drown your not-sorrows in a wildlife documentary?" I offered. Jo loved watching animals even more than she loved the Food Network.

She perked up. "You don't have to leave for work?"

"Short shift today."

"Sweeeeeeeeet. Yes." She scooped up Stella, who had jumped onto the granite countertop to meow in my face. I tried not to think about her litter-box paws getting near the food. "Baby pandas?" Jo asked.

"Anything for you."

TEN

EARLY MARCH WAS TURNING OUT TO BE SLOW SEASON at the Shack. The Valentine's Day rush was over, and the sad, leftover sale candy had already been snatched up or tossed. It was still too cold for all but the most hard-core of ice cream eaters, Easter traffic hadn't started yet, and nobody really wanted to buy St. Patrick's Day candy, no matter how many shamrocks Mr. Sugarman painted on the windows. But judging from the jolly profusion of green that had exploded throughout the store, it seemed to be his favorite holiday. Maybe because he kind of looked like a leprechaun.

"You're terrible," Lexa said, barely holding back a giggle, when I suggested as much. We had an hour left to go before close, but the dribble of customers had finally sputtered to a stop. Yesterday, post–panda videos, there had been enough lulls in my only-four-hour shift to allow me to text Aiden almost throughout. We'd made up rules for a game show called *Wheel of Misfortune* and debated how to spend the first billion it earned us. (Him: a round-the-world adventure featuring hot-air balloons, Jet Skis, parasailing, the motorcycle, and an auto-replenishing picnic basket. Me: a private tropical island replete with palm trees, coconuts, seashells, and sand, where we'd swim with dolphins and befriend a baby sloth.) But today's eight hours of drudgery were slow enough to feel glacial, yet just busy enough to keep me from my phone and its respite. I was antsy and cranky and about ready to whip up a screw-all-this float. Even Lexa looked like she'd had enough.

As I washed sticky residue from the Golly Gumdrops station off my hands, the door jingled and I stifled a groan. But when I turned around, my bad mood melted. It was Aiden.

"Well, hello there," Lexa singsonged as I practically cartwheeled toward him. I really couldn't get over how pretty he was.

"Hey." I leaned in for a kiss but he turned and it landed on his jaw.

"Where were you?" he asked.

"Right here," I said. "Working." He knew that. We'd texted earlier, during my lunch break. My joy went murky with confusion, but then he reached out and took my hand.

"You didn't text me back," he said. "I missed you."

"I missed you too," I murmured against his lips. He'd shaved off the stubble and his skin felt thrillingly new.

"Aww, you guys are so cute," Lexa said. A beat of pride pulsed through my chest.

"How much longer is your shift?" Aiden leaned against the counter. "I can stick around if you want to hang after."

I shook my head. "I'm here until six but I have to go right home. Family dinner."

"Skip it."

If only. "Not a chance."

He plucked a chocolate coin from the pot o' gold by the register and flipped it into the air. "Maybe I could steal you out of here a little early." He tossed the coin again. "Lexa, what do you say, can you handle all these customers on your own?" He gestured around the empty store.

I shot Lexa an apologetic glance, wanting her to know she could say no. It was my turn to close up. But she was already waving me away. "I've got it," she said. "You two have fun. I'll punch you out so Mr. Sugarman won't know."

"Really?" I said.

"Really."

"You're the best." I tugged off my apron and grabbed my coat and bag from the back room before she could change her mind. When I returned a few seconds later, Aiden was eating the chocolate coin. I dropped two quarters on the counter to pay for it.

"I've never skipped out on work before," I said as we slipped out the door. I felt fluttery and giddy with sudden freedom.

He slid his arm around my waist. "I'm glad you can't resist me."

I shoved him lightly. "Oh, I can resist."

"Yeah? You sure about that?" He pulled me in for a full-body kiss.

"Positive," I said. But I didn't even try.

* * *

Two hours later, I let myself in the front door of my house and crouched to greet Rufus. "How mad are they?" I whispered as I leaned my forehead against his and scratched behind his soft orange ears. Roo looked soulfully into my eyes and gave a hopeful wag, but we both knew the answer was probably "furious." I shrugged off my coat, unwound my scarf, and went into the dining room to face my fate.

My parents were seated at the table, a bottle of wine and a lid-ded casserole dish between them. "Hello," I said.

Mom set down her wineglass and regarded me coolly. "Where have you been? We expected you home forty-five minutes ago."

I tried to look surprised. "You didn't get my text?"

Her head jerked slightly. "What text?" I wished I had been smart enough to send one. I should have known I would be late. I should have anticipated I would get lost in the kissing and talking and talking and kissing. I honestly hadn't realized how swiftly the time had passed.

"The text about staying late. Mr. Sugarman asked me to help out with inventory."

My mother looked at my father. "No, we did not get your text," he said. I could tell they didn't quite believe me.

"Oh. It must not have gone through." I took out my phone and fumbled around with it. "Look, I can show you, I sent it around four. He asked me to stay late because he's noticed I'm very responsible and he wants to train me in a few more tasks. He said he thinks I might be junior manager material, if I want to stay on and work full-time through the summer."

Mom looked skeptical but my father perked right up. "Junior manager? That's great. Is there a raise involved?"

"I think two dollars an hour. But not until summer."

Dad nodded sharply. "Ask for three."

Mom sighed. She sounded tired. Well, maybe she would be less exhausted if she spent less energy telling everyone else what to do all the time. "Put away your phone and wash up for dinner. Your father set the table for you tonight, but I hope you realize more responsibility at work doesn't mean your obligations at home disappear."

Of course it didn't. "Thanks, Dad," I said, fleeing to the bathroom before my luck ran out. *We're disappointed in you* could too easily turn into *and you're grounded*, but I seemed to have gotten away with it. I was pretty good at this fibbing thing. Kyle would be proud.

I washed my hands and splashed water on my face, checking my reflection as I patted my cheeks dry. My lips felt swollen from all of Aiden's kisses but the only sign of our make-out session was the happiness radiating out of me.

I hung up the hand towel and took one last glance at the mirror. I looked like a girl who was falling in love.

ELEVEN

"SO." CICILY SNAPPED HER GUM AND GAVE ME A pointed look. "You and Mr. Motorcycle. What is the deal."

"Hmm?" I said. As if I would tell Cicily anything. I had learned that lesson way back in seventh grade, when she extracted the confession that I'd sucked my thumb until, like, age ten, pinkie-swore never to tell another soul on earth, then revealed it to a roomful of girls the next weekend and expected me to somehow laugh along. She was basically a human snake, but with no apple in it for any of us.

"C'mon, spill." She leaned against the locker next to mine, boxing me in and completely ignoring OJ, who was standing there waiting to get inside it. "Everyone's talking about it. I heard Ty is super pissed. He thinks you're rubbing the rebound in his face."

"He does?" I blurted, before remembering Cicily's word should never be taken as truth and Tyson didn't matter. He certainly hadn't looked pissed when I had passed him in the hallway earlier. For the first time in weeks, he'd even given a little nod to acknowledge my existence. But I wasn't scrambling for those scraps of approval anymore. "Whatever. Ty can think what he wants. He's irrelevant to me."

"Amen," Jo said, coming up behind me.

"Mm-hmm." Cicily clearly was not convinced.

"Excuse me," OJ ventured, trying to angle toward her locker.

Cicily didn't budge. "So this new guy. Aiden. Is he in college? He looks older."

OJ shifted her books and opened her mouth, then closed it again. I wished she would bulldoze through and send Cicily flying. "He's nineteen," I said, ignoring the other half of the question. "You know, you're blocking OJ's locker."

"Oh!" Cicily bowed out of the way with a sweep of her arm. "Sooooo sorry, OJ."

OJ glared like this was somehow my fault. I considered whether to tell her that her shirt was buttoned wrong or if that might cause her to breathe fire.

"Kind of a big change for you, huh?" Cicily pressed. Her nostrils flared like she was sniffing for blood. "I mean, Ty is so clean-cut and preppy, and this guy seems really . . . different." Not for the first time, I wondered if Cicily had a thing for Ty. Well, she was welcome to him.

"He is," I said. "He's completely different. To be honest, Tyson wasn't my type. He's great and all, but I was never that into him." It wasn't fully true, but I hoped it would get back to him. I definitely hadn't liked him the way I liked Aiden, and I for sure wasn't Tyson's type. Tyson's type was himself. He hadn't wanted me, he'd wanted a female fan club, evidently one with multiple members.

Aiden didn't have Tyson's debate-tournament trophies, expensive clothes, or Nottingham Terrace pedigree, but none of that stuff mattered. My family wasn't wealthy or perfect either. When Aiden looked at me, I felt wanted. I felt noticed. I felt like the luckiest girl in the world, and the *only* girl in his world. Remembering the lazy, arrogant way Ty had pursued me, and how I'd lapped up his lukewarm attention, I was embarrassed now for us both.

"Is the interrogation over?" Jo asked. "I want french fries."

"Me too." I shut my locker. "See you later, Cee. And hey, OJ, your shirt's misbuttoned." I turned my back on OJ's scowl and followed Jo down the hall, savoring our impending freedom. One more Monday down, fourteen to go before we graduated and escaped this place forever. But first there would be french fries and a milkshake at Bob's Diner, while we waited for Eric to finish his group project for Spanish so he could take us home in the Wildebeest.

"Do you think she was born that way?" Jo mused as we walked toward the exit.

"Who, OJ?" I pictured a pissed-off, snarling baby, though more likely she grew into her anger with puberty.

OJ had arrived at Franklin Magnet Middle School already sporting significant breasts, and I remembered more than one classmate thinking her body was somehow their business. That would have raised my defenses too.

"Cicily."

"Yes, Cicily was definitely born obnoxious."

But Jo was feeling charitable. "She's not obnoxious. She's just nosy and oblivious."

"And that's obnoxious."

Jo pushed open the door and I took a blast of cold air to the face. The distant promise of summer was so much sweeter now that it had Aiden in it. Instead of being the last real summer of Jo and me, this would be the first summer of me with him. "You still haven't forgiven her for what she said at Kacey Hill's sleepover," Jo said.

"I have not," I confirmed. "And she still hasn't noticed."

"You hold a grudge like an elephant."

"I do not!" I said. Jo laughed. "Okay, I do. But she had no right to share that. I got called Thumbelina for the rest of seventh grade."

"All two weeks of it."

"Whatever. She's still dead to me."

"And thus, to me," Jo declared, and even though this was old news, I still felt glad of it.

"Also it was unacceptable and gross how she clearly had a crush on my brother," I said. "Friends' brothers should be off-limits."

"Friends' brothers *are* off-limits," Jo said. She hooked her arm through mine.

As we stepped off the curb to cut through the faculty parking lot, my phone buzzed with a text. I paused and checked the screen. **On your left**

I looked and there was Aiden, leaning against Ralph at the

edge of the senior lot. "Jo!" I said. She was already two cars ahead of me. She turned to see what I was grinning about. "Come on, you can finally meet him."

Jo patted her hair, pretending to primp. "How do I look?" she joked.

"Gorgeous," I replied, but my eyes were already on Aiden's. Even from a hundred feet away, he pulled me in like a magnet trained on my heart. "Hey," I said as we reached him.

"Hey." He kissed me. "Surprise." He nudged my nose with his own.

Jo cleared her throat. I'd almost forgotten she was with me. "Sorry," I said, pulling away from his lips. "Aiden, this is Jo. Jo, this is Aiden. And Ralph," I added, touching the bike.

She snorted out a laugh. "Ralph, like the penis?"

Aiden and I stared at her.

"*Forever*? Judy Blume?" Aiden shook his head and Jo chortled. "It's basically synonymous with dick," she said.

I issued a cease-and-desist with my eyes. Making fun of the motorcycle was not good.

She pulled herself together. "Never mind. Pleased to meet you." She stuck out her hand.

He shook it. "Likewise."

A beat passed in silence, then Aiden turned to me. "So . . . shall we?" He lifted his helmet. Jo's eyebrows shot up.

"Oh," I said, looking at both their expectant faces. "I can't. I promised Jo—we're going to get french fries. At the diner down the street."

Aiden's expression didn't change but I felt a wave of disappointment roll off him and crash into me. *I'm sorry. I'd rather go with you*, I tried to tell him with telepathy. But I couldn't ditch Jo. Not again.

"Come with us," Jo offered, before I could think to do the same.

Aiden hesitated and for a second I was certain he would say no, but he shrugged. "Sure. I like french fries."

"Cool," Jo said, and the knots inside me unraveled. This was perfect, actually. I felt weirdly grateful to them both.

Aiden locked up his helmet and we set off toward Bob's. Jo led the way and I fell into step beside her, before realizing the sidewalk wasn't wide enough for three. I slowed my pace to kind of hover in between them, but Aiden reached out and took my hand. He laced his fingers through mine and pulled me to his side.

Jo glanced back but didn't comment. It was a short walk, anyway.

We followed her down East North Street, past the flow of student cars escaping the school parking lot. The sidewalk was gritty beneath the soles of my sneakers and Aiden's lace-up boots. I liked the sound of the *crunch* our feet made with each step— the rhythm of us.

"God, I would kill for it to be spring." Jo spun around to walk backward so she could face us. "What do we need to sacrifice, and to which goddess, to make this winter finally end?"

Winters in our corner of western New York were fifty shades of gray, none of them alluring, except when it was pitch-black or snowing. And this year we'd had barely any snow—just cold, dampness, and ice. Jo had already declared it the most depressing winter on record two months before, and we still had a few weeks left before the grays would shift to browns. It was hard to even imagine the green that might follow. But it hadn't been bothering me so much in the past week. Now that winter contained picnics, lake walks, and Aiden, it seemed nearly as beautiful as autumn.

"We could try sacrificing Stella," I suggested, and at the look in Jo's eyes, instantly regretted it. "She'd still have eight more lives," I added to soften it.

Jo huffed and turned back around, but I knew she'd already forgiven me. Besides, now we were even for her comments about Ralph.

Aiden squeezed my hand. "I don't like cats either," he said. I wouldn't have defined myself that way—I loved all animals, even Stella, my nemesis—but I squeezed back.

When we got to Bob's Diner it was mostly empty as usual. The two fast-food places down the road got a lot more after-school traffic. At this hour, Bob's was typically only patronized by old men, Jo, and me, plus sometimes Eric if it wasn't soccer season. I wasn't sure I had ever seen another teenager inside.

I watched Aiden take it all in as we followed Jo to our red, saggy booth in the back. "Is this okay?" I asked, suddenly worried he might be annoyed I had dragged him along. I didn't yet know him well enough to tell if his quietness was normal or sulky.

"Sure," he said. "I mean, I'd rather have you all to myself, but it's fine. Smells like they've got coffee."

"They do." Not that I had ever ordered that.

We slid into the booth and released ourselves from our winter layers. Jo and I did, anyway. Aiden kept on his leather jacket and flagged the waitress. She wiped off our table with a cloth that smelled like fake lemon and bleach, and plopped down three menus. "Anything to drink?"

"Coffee," Aiden said. "Black."

"Me too."

Jo gave me a little smirk, which I ignored. "I'll have some too. With cream, please," she said.

"You got it." The waitress turned away.

Aiden put his hand on my leg and pressed gently. "There's nothing hotter than a woman who takes her coffee pure." The warmth of his touch shot through me.

"Oh?" Jo said. The waitress returned with three mugs in one hand and a coffeepot in the other. Jo picked up two sugar packets from the collection on the table, shook them, ripped the tops, and tipped them both into her cup at once. The waitress poured.

"I'll be right back with that cream, hon."

Jo smiled. "Thank you."

Aiden picked up the menu with his free hand. "What's good here?"

"We always get fries and a milkshake," I said. "I'm not sure they even serve anything else."

"The milkshakes are the perfect consistency for fry-dipping," Jo explained. "Not too thin, not too thick. So you get the best combination of salty plus sweet and hot plus cold."

"That's . . . weird," Aiden said. "I think I'll try the burger."

Jo shrugged. "Your loss."

We placed our order and I sipped my coffee, watching Jo stir in her cream. It tasted a bit burnt—definitely not as good as the other coffee I'd been drinking lately—but no way was I reaching for the sugar after that comment from Aiden. I reminded myself that I liked it this way, and took another sip.

Under the table, Aiden's thumb made slow circles on my thigh. I tried to focus on what Jo was saying, but his touch was too distracting. All I could process was his hand caressing my leg and the way my body buzzed from wanting more.

Maybe I should have apologized to Jo in the parking lot and let Aiden whisk me away. By now he could be pressing the whole length of his body against mine, running his hands up my sides as he kissed my neck and jaw and lips, as he had done last night after my shift. I wanted that so badly it was hard to see straight.

In that moment, I knew: I was going to sleep with him.

The waitress dropped our plates in front of us and Aiden lifted his hand from my leg, releasing me from his spell. I wondered how many people he'd had sex with. Probably at least two. I tried not to be jealous of whoever they were. It was good if he was experienced. But I would be responsible and ask him to get tested first, and we would use condoms, of course. If I was ready to have sex, I needed to be ready to have that conversation. And despite never even really considering doing it in those months with Ty—I'd always thought, before this, that

I would wait until college, when I was no longer living in my parents' house, no longer subject to their rules, and that I'd date the guy for at least a semester first—with Aiden I was ready. He was the One.

I dipped a fry in the chocolate milkshake Jo and I were splitting, and popped it into my mouth before the ice cream could drip off. Jo and I locked eyes and smiled as we both chewed and swallowed. It really was the perfect combination.

"How's the burger?" I asked Aiden. He was already halfway through it.

"Decent," he said. "Want a bite?"

"No thanks."

Jo dipped three fries at once. "Betts doesn't eat red meat," she said.

Aiden almost choked in surprise. "What? Not even bacon?"

I shook my head. "No bacon." Bacon had been the first thing to go. Jo and Eric and I had given it up together after watching *Babe: Pig in the City* when we were eight.

"Hmm," he said, putting his hand back on my leg. "I'm not sure I can trust someone who doesn't like bacon."

"So you're anti-Semitic?" Jo said. I wanted to kick her. That obviously wasn't what Aiden had meant and her family wasn't kosher. But Jo had never met a confrontation she didn't like. "I'm Jewish, by the way. And a full vegetarian, just in case Betts didn't warn you. Highly untrustworthy."

"I didn't know Asians could be Jewish," Aiden said.

I cringed but Jo looked at him evenly. "My dad's family is

Jewish. My mom's family is Thai. Ta-da: Asian Jew."

"Cool," Aiden said, and they dropped it.

The seconds ticked by. Aiden finished his burger. Jo watched me add salt to the fries. I avoided her eyes but felt them boring into me. For some reason, she was determined not to make this easy.

I wasn't prepared for that. When I had pictured introducing them, I never imagined it might be awkward. I had no precedent for how to respond. Jo and Ty hadn't exactly been BFFs but they always managed to keep up a steady stream of banter and seemed to at least find each other somewhat entertaining. I knew Aiden wasn't as open with most people as he was with me, but usually Jo could talk to anyone. It sucked that she was barely trying.

My brain flailed for a way to prompt them into conversation and bonding. It came up blank. I felt like he was oil and she was water and someone had stolen my whisk: It was futile to even try mixing them together. I would only end up making a bigger mess.

"More coffee?" the waitress asked, coming by with the pot.

"Nah, just the check." Aiden took out his wallet and removed two tens and a five. When the waitress set down our bill, he put the money on top and said, "I got it."

Jo scooped up a spoonful of milkshake. We'd barely made a dent in it. "Thanks?"

"You're welcome." He turned to me. "You ready?"

I put down the fry I was holding. "Um, yeah." I wrapped my scarf around my neck and looked at Jo as Aiden stood. "Is this okay? Do you want me to stay until Eric gets here? I thought Aiden could give me a ride home." This clearly wasn't fun for anyone, but that didn't make it cool for me to leave her.

Jo held my gaze for a few hard seconds, then sighed. "Sure. Do your thing."

I hesitated, but Jo pulled the milkshake toward her and waved me away. "Don't worry. I'm not crying. This is just diner grease on my face."

I grinned my appreciation and scooted out of the booth. "Tasty. I'll text you later." I slid on my coat and walked toward Aiden, who was waiting for me at the door.

TWELVE

AS SOON AS WE STEPPED OUT INTO THE PARKING LOT, Aiden's lips were on mine, his hands pulling my already-pressed-to-his hips in closer, closer. He sucked my lower lip, biting it gently, and teased my tongue with his. I exhaled and pushed him away. "Let's go someplace more private," I said.

I laughed as he charged off down the street, yanking me along behind him. We broke into a run, still holding hands and laughing, until we were forced to slow down to catch our breath. He scooped me into another kiss. "You're incredible," he said, and we kissed and panted and smiled goofily into each other's faces. "Come on." We speed-walked back to Ralph. "How long do we have before you need to be home?"

I checked my phone. "An hour and a half."

Aiden groaned. "Tomorrow I want you all to myself. The whole afternoon. Can you give me that?"

I nodded with my lips already back on his. My mom usually came home early on Tuesdays, but I would find a way to make it work—tell her I needed to stay late for a project or something. I'd figure it out when my head wasn't spinning from lust. It was hard to focus on anything besides the feel of Aiden's body pressing into mine, the taste of his mouth, the desire to be someplace where we could shed these winter layers and mash our bodies even closer.

Aiden pulled back just far enough to look into my eyes. "Let's get out of here."

"Yes."

Soon my arms were around his chest, the wind roaring in our ears, as we accelerated toward the promise of *more*.

We parked in front of a narrow two-story house with green shutters and a small front porch. Aiden led me to a door on the side of the garage and turned his key in the lock. "Home sweet home," he said, holding it open. I walked up the staircase, heart thrumming with curiosity. I knew Aiden lived in Southside in a studio above his family's garage, where he paid low rent in exchange for helping his dad out with the kids and the yard work, but I hadn't been able to fully picture what his place might be like. "It's open," Aiden said when I reached the door at the top, so I turned the knob and let us in.

The first thing I noticed about Aiden's apartment was how tidy it was. I hadn't been in a lot of teenage boys' abodes, but none of the ones I'd seen had looked anything like this. Tyson's room had been a mess of clothes, sneakers, electronics, empty Doritos bags, debate team fliers and notes and briefs, schoolwork, and miscellany, all tangled in a nest of maleness, imbued with the scent of his cologne. Every once in a while, Ty's mom would bring in fresh laundry and cart out the old, throwing away the more obvious trash while she was in there, but as far as I could tell, Ty himself had never so much as pitched a pop can toward a recycling bin. In retrospect, it was just one of the many less-than-ideal things about him I had somehow overlooked while we were together. Eric's room and my brother Kyle's weren't anywhere near as messy as that, but Aiden still made them both seem like slobs.

The room was sparsely furnished: a mattress spread with a dark blue comforter, a lamp and a squat tower of books on the floor beside it. A desk in one corner with a closed laptop, three pens in a glass jar. Two bowls, one spoon, and a mug drying in the dish rack on the counter in the kitchenette, between the empty sink and the gleaming coffeemaker. A red towel folded over a rack on the bathroom door. A low dresser with a line of paperbacks across the top. Off-white walls with nothing on them.

Aiden tucked his leather jacket onto a hook by the door and nestled up behind me, reaching around to unzip my coat. As he pulled it off my shoulders, he kissed the patch of skin between my scarf and my ear. It was tempting to lean back into him or spin around to put my lips on his, but now that I was in Aiden's home—this place where he slept and ate and read and thought and did who knows what else—I was too curious. All I wanted was to take in every detail.

I shook my arms free from the coat sleeves and stepped toward the fridge, which had a couple of takeout menus—pizza and Greek—a kid's drawing of a pink-and-purple motorcycle under a rainbow, and two school photos stuck to the front with square magnets. "Is this your brother and sister?" I asked.

"Alex and Kendra. He's in fifth grade and she's in third. That's Kendra's portrait of Ralph."

"Pretty good." I peered closer at the girl's gleeful, gap-toothed smile and the boy's serious eyes. "He's like a mini you."

"Yeah, people say that. Kendra looks more like our dad."

He didn't mention how their mother factored into that family equation, so I didn't ask. "Some people think my brother and I look alike, but I don't see it," I said. "My face shape is round and his is long. But we don't really look like our parents, either."

"Well, if your brother looks like you, he must be beautiful."

I turned to hide my blush. No one had ever called me beautiful before—no one besides my grandmother, anyway. Tyson had once grunted that a skirt I was wearing looked hot, and sometimes someone said my hair looked nice or they liked my shoes, but hearing a boy like Aiden use a word like that, referring to me—even in a sentence that was weirdly about Kyle—made me realize how deeply I wanted him to believe it. "Thanks," I managed. I glanced at the mini library on top of the dresser. *Into Thin Air. Slaughterhouse-Five. Selected Poems of Rumi. Zen and the Art of Motorcycle Maintenance.* "You have a lot of books. I wasn't expecting that."

"Just because I'm a dropout doesn't mean I'm illiterate," he said.

I whirled around. "I didn't mean—"

"Relax. I'm kidding." His hand swept the room. "Go ahead.

It's clear you're dying to poke around. I'm afraid the books are about all there is to look at."

"Well, you know what they say: 'Look at a man's bookshelf, see a window into his soul.'"

"Yeah? Who says that?"

"I dunno. Taylor Swift?" I crouched to examine the stack near his bed. I loved being here, loved that he was letting me snoop around. "So then what does it mean that your books aren't on shelves?"

"I guess I have no soul. I'm like the Tin Man," he said.

"The Tin Man has no heart. I don't think they get into souls in *The Wizard of Oz*."

"Oh. Then I guess it means I haven't gotten around to building a shelf."

On the Road. Juliet, Naked. The Catcher in the Rye. Infinite Jest. For Whom the Bell Tolls. I touched the spine of *The Amazing Adventures of Kavalier & Clay*. That was one of Eric's favorite books but he had warned me not to read it because the dog in it dies. "Jo would ask why you don't have any books by women."

"Maybe Jo should pull the stick out of her butt."

I winced but I knew I'd deserved that. It was insensitive to have even mentioned it, especially after the way things had gone at the diner. And it was true that Jo was judgmental. I was so used to it I hardly ever noticed, but I definitely had noticed today. No wonder Aiden was on edge. "I'm sorry," I said.

"No, you caught me," he said. "I may seem like a nice guy but I'm actually a sexist pig. I'm glad I brought you here so you could see the real me."

I stood up, fast. "That's not what I meant."

"Yeah, well, that's what it sounded like."

I put my hand on his arm. He stiffened but didn't pull away. "I'm sorry. I just . . . it was a stupid thing to say. Please don't be mad. I'm really sorry." I moved closer, right into the waves of his anger. I didn't want us to be fighting. I wanted us to be kissing. "Forgive me?"

Aiden looked straight at me and gave my chest a tap. I held still. He moved his hand to my chin and held it for a long moment, before pulling my face roughly toward his. Our lips smashed together and his tongue pushed into my mouth as I kissed back with equal parts apology and desire.

He pulled back suddenly. "I don't care what your friends think. They have nothing to do with you and me. All that matters is us."

I nodded, breathless, and he kissed me again. This time I was the one to pull away. "Aiden," I said, willing myself not to chicken out. I needed him to know this. "I think I'm falling in love with you."

"Good," he said, "because I've already fallen deep."

THIRTEEN

WHEN DAD DROPPED ME OFF AT SCHOOL THE NEXT morning, the Wildebeest was already parked in the senior lot and Jo was rummaging through my locker. I came up behind her, antennae on alert. "I keep the porn in my Latin folder. Top shelf," I said.

Jo turned. "I need lip balm. Desperately." I took some Burt's from my bag and held it out to her, searching for signs of residual irritation. Her radio silence last night post-diner had been unusual but not unheard of, and to be fair I hadn't texted her either, though maybe I should have. She yanked off the cap, smeared on several coats, and sighed. "Thank you. Amazing. God, I am so sick of winter." She stepped aside so I could shove my belongings into the locker. I relaxed. We were fine, as we should be.

"It's almost spring. You'll make it." I pulled out *Their Eyes Were Watching God* and my notebook for Modern American Lit.

"Thanks, Pollyanna." Jo leaned against the locker bank, then jumped, startling me. "Guess what? I got my road-test date."

"Awesome. When?"

"Six weeks. April twentieth. What if I pass?"

"Then you'll be licensed to drive," I said. "What do you mean, what if you pass?" I tucked my scarf out of the way before shutting the locker door, careful not to jostle the dial. If I never spun it, it never locked, a trick I had learned from Kyle freshman year. For the first two years of high school, his locker had been right across from mine. I'd felt monitored at times, having my brother so close by, but there were moments now when I missed glancing over there and seeing him. It stank how thoroughly he'd abandoned me to only-childdom. He wasn't even coming home for spring break.

Jo twirled in a dreamy circle as we set off down the hall. "It feels like the end of an era, you know? Three more months of high school, one last summer of the Way Things Were, and then boom. No more riding around in the Wildebeest with the radio blasting and all of us singing along like a cheesy movie montage of carefree teenage happiness. Soon we'll be at college, with separate soundtracks and separate lives. All I've wanted for four years was for high school to end, but I'm not ready. I don't want everything about us to change. It's already changing."

"Um, okay," I said, "but failing your test won't stop time. You can't extend our adolescence by refusing to get a license. You'll just become a grown-up who still can't drive without adult supervision." I was glad to hear her sounding wistful and overdramatic about the future, though. Usually when she talked about Life After High School it was a series of exciting plans that she barely seemed to notice wouldn't include me. Although at least after college, once her bakery got famous and her cookbooks were bestsellers and she'd landed her own show on the Food Network, I'd get to see her every week on TV.

"Who needs to drive? That's what ride-share apps are for." But I knew her parents and Eric had already given her that lecture. "You'll do great," I assured her. "Remember: gas on the right, brake on the left. And if you back into a pole, just say it's the pole's fault. They can't fail you for that." Jo had taken driver's ed back when Eric did, three years ago, but she never showed the slightest interest in driving, to the point where she hadn't even shown up for her first road test. Like some part of her had decided that since Eric had a license, she didn't need or want one of her own. But now things were really changing. Even they would be moving apart. "You may want to bring bribes, though, just in case things go wrong."

I expected an elbow to the ribs, but Jo's attention was already elsewhere. I looked in the direction she was staring and saw what had distracted her: Sydney.

"They're not anything serious," Jo said as Sydney rose up on tiptoe to meet Benji's kiss. He ran his hands down her body and I felt a deep, sudden pang of missing Aiden. Seven more hours before I would get to see him and already I was jumpy with anticipation.

"You think?" I said carefully as we walked past the PDA. They looked plenty serious to me, but clearly that was not what Jo wanted to hear.

"I know. She told me last night."

"Wait, what?" I grabbed Jo's arm and she broke into a grin.

"Yeah. We were texting a little. She said it's fun for now but she could never seriously date someone who thinks dolphins are reptiles and spells 'stupid' with two Os."

"Since when do you have her number?"

Jo was practically skipping. "Since yesterday. She was drawing these incredible narwhals in math and we started talking about them and I was like, 'Give me your number,' and she did."

"Wow." I was impressed but not surprised. Jo had always been the kind of girl who makes things happen. She had guts.

"I was going to tell you at the diner but then Aiden was there."

Just the sound of his name made my heart beam. "So what did you think?"

She shrugged and my happy glow dimmed. "Hard to say. I barely got to meet him."

"Oh, come on."

Jo shifted her books to her other arm. "He's definitely your type."

"Meaning what, exactly?" I asked, not sure I wanted to know. It hadn't sounded like a compliment.

"You have a thing for assholes."

I stopped walking.

"Beeeeeee. Don't be mad. You know it's a little bit true."

I stared at the laughing foxes on her shirt. "Aiden is nothing like Tyson."

"Sure," she said. "No, you're right, I'm sorry. I'm sure he's great.

He was just—I'd expected him to be a little more interested in meeting your best friend, that's all, and I guess I took it personally. But he clearly adores you. As he should."

I stood still, trying to process all that, as the flow of students streamed around us. The shirt-foxes blurred all together into one, then separated back into *fox fox fox fox fox*. The bell rang.

"Just . . . hos before bros, you know?" Jo said. I didn't smile.

"Why can't you be happy for me?" I asked, but I already knew the answer. She was jealous. Even when I'd been with Ty, Jo had always come first. She wasn't used to sharing me. Well, she would have to adjust.

"I am happy for you, Betts. And where you go, I go. But you guys ditched me, like, ten fries in. Look, let's do it again sometime when he's got more than eight seconds to spend wolfing down his burger and waxing holy about bacon and then rushing you out the door. Okay?"

The second bell rang. We really had to get to class. And I couldn't take those stupid foxes one second longer. "Okay," I said, letting her off the hook. Jo looked relieved.

Aiden's words from yesterday pulsed through my veins. *All that matters is us.*

FOURTEEN

BY LUNCHTIME THINGS WITH JO RETURNED TO NOR-
mal, at least on the surface. I had decided to let it go—or to not
continue it, anyway. If Jo needed some time to adjust to Aiden,
then fine. My being in love by definition excluded her, and I got
why she might be slow to accept that. She would warm up to him
eventually, and he to her, and in the meantime, we both would
pretend this incident hadn't happened. Neither of us wanted to
be fighting, so we wouldn't. Simple.

We invoked Jo's firstborn twin privileges to cut Eric in the
lunch line and joked around with him about the "special sauce"
for the meatloaf none of us would be eating, though most likely
no actual meat was involved. Once we had our food, Eric went
off to sit with his soccer friends while Jo and I snagged end seats
at a table with some girls we'd been friendly-but-never-quite-
friends with since early sophomore year. They wanted details
on Aiden and me, and when Eleanor asked Jo if she'd met him
yet, Jo said "of course" and launched into a raunchy description

of his physical attributes in an attempt to make me blush. It worked.

I sculpted the glob of mashed potatoes on my tray into a heart and imagined how I would describe it all to Aiden later on: The straight-faced, confiding way Jo said the words "love sausage." Eleanor's widening blue eyes, which matched the elastics on her second round of braces. Krystal's high-pitched, rapid-fire laugh that always took me by surprise.

A roar went up from across the room and I swiveled just in time to see a tower of milk cartons that had been balancing on top of Tyson's head topple to the floor, exploding at the feet of three other guys on the debate team. Tyson whooped. "New record!" he shouted, and I flashed on the time he'd laid his head on my lap, emitted a loud fake snore, and interrupted what I was saying with a cutting "Good news, you've cured my insomnia." Hilarious.

I turned back to my table. "So spontaneous," Jo said.

"You've definitely traded up," Krystal told me.

I agreed, but Ty was irrelevant. His jokey insults would never slice through me again. And Aiden wouldn't dream of disrespecting me that way. As I half listened to a story about something Eleanor had heard about or maybe seen happen in the locker room but Krystal was certain wasn't true, I glanced around the cafeteria, viewing it all through the Lens of Him. The Aiden voice in my head said, *It's so high school*, and we shared a secret smile. This was no longer my world. He was.

But I didn't tell Aiden about any of it when we were finally together, sitting on his bed, arms and legs entwined. All the tidbits and minutiae I'd been collecting for him throughout the day scattered from my thoughts as Aiden kissed me slowly, sweetly, with a gentleness that made me fierce with want. I kept it contained but it was hard not to devour him.

He slid his hands up my arms, along my shoulders, down the length of my sides and around my hips, and finally just under the hem of my shirt. "Is this okay?" he said, his touch light against the skin of my back.

"Yes." I pulled my shirt off over my head. "Is this okay?" I asked.

Aiden drew a sharp breath and pulled me closer. He kissed a line across my collarbone and slid the bra straps off my shoulders. I shivered and tugged at his T-shirt. "It's only fair if we match," I said. He smiled, and in an instant his shirt was on the floor on top of mine. He leaned back against the pillows, pulling me down with him, and I leaned into the niceness of skin on skin, warm and soft and wonderful. I ran my fingers up his stomach and through his surprise patch of chest hair—Tyson hadn't had any. I liked it. I liked everything about him.

Jo was so wrong.

I channeled all my courage and asked without preamble, "How many people have you slept with?"

He kissed my nose. "Zero."

I pulled back to see if he was teasing. Of all the answers I had been steeling myself for, that one hadn't occurred to me as a possibility. "Really?"

"Really. Why, how many people have you slept with?" he asked, sitting up a bit.

"Zero," I said.

"Cool."

I tried to keep my voice steady. "I want you to be my first."

He tucked my hair behind my ear and cupped his hand behind my neck. "I want you to be my only."

FIFTEEN

WE DIDN'T DO IT RIGHT AWAY. HE DIDN'T HAVE ANY condoms and I didn't want it to feel rushed, so we decided we'd wait until Friday, when we could take our time and "do it properly," as Aiden said, his face serious, though I couldn't stop my own grin. Still, there was plenty we *could* do without condoms involved, and soon the grin was all I was wearing.

All week I was buzzing with it: anticipation mixed with curiosity, adrenaline, and nerves. We were going to do it. We were going to have sex. And from that moment on, there would be no turning back. Whether or not we were each other's forever, we would always be each other's first—permanently linked in this impalpable way, no matter what came next. It was a bond and a promise I couldn't wait to make.

I went through the motions of my week—homework; Sugar Shack; walking Rufus in the rain, walking Rufus in the snow, walking Rufus through the slushy, frozen mix; setting the table, washing dishes, getting through dinner with my parents; talking with Jo, joking with Eric, avoiding Cicily's probing and OJ's wrath—all of it a haze except in those sharp moments when Aiden texted and suddenly I felt present and alive.

If Jo noticed anything was up, she didn't comment, and I didn't tell her what Aiden and I were planning. I didn't tell her much about him at all. It was weird how almost not-weird it was to block her out of this huge decision, but I didn't want to hear any more of her opinions about him, and really, it was none of her business. Besides, she was plenty wrapped up in her own concerns.

Friday morning, she threw herself against OJ's locker and heaved a dramatic sigh. I selected a green pen from my pencil case. "What's wrong, pumpkin?" I asked.

Jo groaned. "Yesterday Sydney and I got in this adorable fight about which is the better ingredient, garlic or ginger. Which, ginger, obviously."

I nodded. "Obviously."

"So last night I baked these triple-ginger biscotti to help prove my point and I was going to give them to her at break with a cup of Darjeeling but now *look at my face.*"

I looked at it. "What?"

"My nose! It's all dried out and irritated from stupid fucking winter and it feels like a giant zit is about to erupt out my nostril and take over my face. I look disgusting."

"Move your hand," I said. "Hold still, let me see."

Jo tipped her head back. I inspected her nostrils. They were a little bit red, but only from nose-blowing. "It's fine. You're totally fine."

"It's not fine. It's red and puffy and flaky and gross and she's going to think I have nasal herpes."

"Okay, *that's* gross."

She moaned and hid her face in my shoulder. "No one will ever want to make out with me again."

"I always want to make out with you." I pushed her away so I could close my locker door. "But we probably shouldn't share tissues for a while, in case you do have nasal herpes. You'll have to blow your nose on my sleeve instead." I held out my arm.

Her face scrunched up. "Is that even a thing? I mean, I made it up, but what if it's a real thing?"

"Nasal herpes? I don't even want to know," I said, trying not to picture it.

Jo shuddered. "Let's swear we'll never google it."

"We do not need those images in our pretty little heads." If there was one thing we had learned in our eighth-grade health class, it was Never Ask the Internet Anything.

I had never seen Jo so worked up about a crush. The chances of anything actually happening still seemed slim—I'd had at least two more Syd-and-Benji sightings that week and there had been plenty of face-sucking involved—but of course I was rooting for it. And if Jo fell in love too, maybe she would understand about Aiden.

Then again, maybe not. What Aiden and I had felt so much bigger than any high school relationship, and not just because he was older. I felt almost sorry for Jo that she couldn't possibly fathom the difference. I couldn't have either, before I'd fallen deep into it.

After a lifetime of playing Jo's sidekick, it was strange to suddenly feel leagues ahead of her. This was new territory for us. Ever since the third day of the third week of second grade, that was who I'd been: Jo's best friend. But now I was something different. Now I was Aiden's.

It was sad, in a way, how quickly things were changing, but maybe it was the natural course of things. Despite my apprehension about being apart from Jo, I was excited about SUNY Geneseo—excited for in-state tuition and choosing a major and moving into a residence hall a full, glorious hour and twenty minutes outside my parents' reach, but luckily not all that far, really, from Aiden. It would be easy for him to come out on weekends and stuff if he changed up his shifts at the garage. In a few weeks Jo would get her acceptances from Brown and Swarthmore and probably everywhere else far away she'd applied, and before we knew it, we would be starting down our separate paths and the space between us would be measured in miles instead of moments. I'd simply started down my path a little early.

We walked toward homeroom. "So my parents are meeting Aiden tonight."

Jo's eyes went wide. "What did you tell them?"

"That I met him through Lexa and this is our first date." It was true enough. That day at the Sugar Shack, he'd been talking to her first.

"Are you nervous?"

Yes, but not about that. "No. They liked Tyson just fine and he's a dick."

"Fair point. And I guess you won't be mentioning he's a drop-out who rides a motorcycle," she said. My face flashed hot with annoyance, but she was right—instead I'd told them he was out of high school and "taking a gap year." Still, it didn't even seem to occur to her I might find her comment insulting. She kept talking right past it. "You guys should come over and watch a movie. I'll make peanut-butter popcorn."

"I think Aiden has something planned," I said. I tried to look sorry.

Jo tried not to look hurt. "You're still coming over tomorrow, though, right?"

"Yup, after my shift."

"Cool." We stopped outside my classroom. I suddenly felt very tired. "Hey, Betts?"

"Yeah?"

"I really am glad for you. About Aiden. And I want a chance to get to know him, okay? You're my best friend. I want to be part of your life."

"I know." I did not want to have this conversation in the hallway, eight seconds before class. I didn't want to have this conversation at all. Jo and I never fought, not about important things. We'd always been on the same page, the same team. It was exhausting to feel so very differently about this. I didn't know how to tell her that what she thought of him didn't matter, that this part of my life didn't involve her. Everything between Aiden and me was wrapped up in its own cocoon. The Cocoon of Us held something infinite, but it didn't have space for anyone else.

Everything I needed was inside.

I changed the subject. "You should give her the biscotti. She'll love it. I gotta go."

Confusion flashed across Jo's face as I backed toward the door. "What? Oh. Thanks. Okay."

We both turned away.

SIXTEEN

IT WAS A SURREAL MOMENT, CHOOSING WHAT OUTFIT to put on for my last few hours as a virgin. My underwear collection was not exactly curated for these purposes, I realized as I stood in my towel, poking through the drawer of value-pack cotton, thirty-eight minutes before Aiden was supposed to arrive. Perhaps I should have shopped for the occasion.

I pulled out my nicest bra (black, a little lacy), gave it the sniff test (deodorant-y but fine), and paired it with red cotton underpants. My brain flashed on Jo and Eric in their kitchen last fall, saying the word "panties" back and forth in snooty British accents à la Alan Rickman as Snape, while their mother laughed and their father shook his head and grinned into his coffee. Not how my parents would have reacted, at all. My mom would have shut that joke down with one look, before it started. Her presence did not inspire fun.

I hoped she would be chill in front of Aiden tonight and not launch into one of her lectures or interrogations. If I could get him out of the house before that happened, the encounter would be a win.

It would be fine either way, though. Aiden could hold his own in whatever conversation might come up, and he'd said he didn't mind that my parents were protective and I wasn't allowed to date him until they'd met him. Once we'd made it through those first few minutes of parental scrutiny, we would escape into our perfect evening. And after tonight I could stop hiding his existence—though of course we would still have to keep the motorcycle under wraps.

In the shower I'd been envisioning an outfit involving my jean skirt, patterned tights, and the purple lace-up boots Jo had talked me into buying on super sale last summer (they were perfect for her but only came in my size), but as I pictured Aiden undressing me later (distracting, delicious thought), I realized tights might not be the best choice. Scrunching them off in front of him seemed awkward at best, and if he tugged them off for me I would be worried they might rip. Better to go with jeans for easier removal.

I chose a fitted black tank and a soft gray sweater and pulled them on, thrilling at the knowledge that when I did so again a few hours later, I would be irreversibly different. Not that I bought into any of that societal crap about virginity or purity—one more way the world tries to police women's bodies—but I did believe in the power of experiences, and tonight Aiden and I would be experiencing something incredibly important, for the first time, together. That meant something. It was kind of a huge freaking deal.

I checked my reflection in the mirror above my dresser. I felt proud and excited about this choice I was making. I felt powerful, responsible, and ready.

I had a sudden urge to call Jo and tell her what I was planning. But just as quickly, the inclination passed. She was probably busy making dinner with her dad, and there were only a few minutes before Aiden would get here. And in truth I was still smarting from that thing she'd said earlier. Besides, I already had someone to share this experience with: him.

Rufus barked, and seconds later the doorbell rang. My heart jumped as I lunged for my socks, glancing at the clock. He was seven minutes early.

"I'll get it!" I yelled, shoving my feet into the nearest pair of shoes and rushing out into the hallway. Aiden shouldn't have to face my parents for the first time alone. But as I reached the top of the stairs, I saw my father already holding open the door and Aiden shaking his hand as he stepped through it, saying, "Nice to meet you, sir." Rufus sniffed at his legs, tail wagging, as Aiden looked up and his eyes locked on mine. I started down the stairs and watched the slow, sexy smile spread across his face. He looked amazing.

"Hello, Aiden," my mother called. She emerged from the kitchen, wiping her hands on a dish towel, and Aiden turned her way.

I felt a thousand rapid-fire heartbeats in the length of their pause.

Mom pulled back her shoulders. "Oh. What a surprise."

"Nice to see you again, Ms. Jensen."

I hurried down the last few steps on high alert. Jensen was Mom's maiden name, which she still used professionally to "maintain privacy" at school. I stood next to Aiden. "You guys have met?"

He kept his eyes on my mother. Neither of them blinked. "We have," she said.

My father cleared his throat. He looked as clueless as I felt. "Well," he said, gesturing toward the living room. Nobody moved.

"What have you been doing with yourself these past few years, Aiden?" my mother asked.

Aiden lifted his chin. "Working hard and staying out of trouble," he said. "I'm fixing cars at Percy's Garage over on South Park Ave, learning a ton from Percy and the guys. I earned my GED last summer and I'm thinking of applying for community college this fall." He was? That was news to me. I looked back and forth between them. Aiden's face was earnest and open. My mother's face was stone. "I've been spending a lot of time with my little brother and sister, too. Helping my dad where I can. Family is very important to me," he added.

"Helping is good," my father said. They ignored him.

Mom stared Aiden down like he was a stain on her favorite blouse. Her eyes narrowed slightly as she seemed to reach a decision. We all waited to hear it.

She looked at me. "You have your phone charged?" I nodded. "And enough money for a cab ride home if you need it?" I nodded again. "Good." She didn't smile. "I want you home before ten."

I started to protest—my normal Friday night curfew was

eleven—but Aiden cut me off with a firm "No problem."

"Where are you kids off to?" Dad said.

His place, I thought, and almost wished I could say it. Despite this charade, my parents did not own me.

"I thought we might try the rink at Canalside, maybe get a bite to eat someplace nearby," Aiden said so smoothly it sounded true. He looked at me. "Do you skate?"

"I skate. And I definitely eat." I grabbed my coat off its hook and reached for the doorknob. "Let's go." *Before my mother changes her mind.*

"Have fun," Dad said. "Be safe."

I thought of the condoms tucked away in my bag. *Safe.* That was the plan. "We will," I said as I pushed Aiden out the door. I pulled it shut behind us, closed my eyes, and exhaled long and hard as my brain followed the strings and connected the dots, producing one tangled mess also known as my life.

Aiden's footsteps crunched in the driveway. He unlocked the passenger-side door and held it open, waiting for me to get inside. I almost hoped my parents were watching.

"Thanks," I said, trying to read his flat expression as I sank down into the seat. The door smacked shut, jolting my heart on impact.

Aiden started the car without a word, backed out of the driveway, and stared straight ahead as he drove. The tension in his jawline matched the tightness in my chest and his white-knuckled grip on the wheel. I felt like I should apologize, but for what? This wasn't something I had done. It was a pathetic impulse, always jumping to apply an "I'm sorry" to things, but helpless and pathetic was how I felt when he iced me out like this.

Aiden slowed for the stop sign at the end of my street, signaled, and turned right. I put my hand on his leg and felt his thigh muscles tense then relax beneath my touch. He dropped one hand off the wheel and covered mine, squeezing it gently. Relief coursed through me. We were still an *us*.

I leaned back in my seat as the heat kicked in and we put more and more distance between ourselves and my parents, lessening their hold with every house we passed. "So my mom was your English teacher," I said. "That sucks."

His lips twisted in a grimace. "Yeah. Didn't see that one coming."

"I'm sorry. I didn't know." Just in case it needed to be said. As much as it felt like Aiden already knew me, that something in him saw and understood the truth of me better than anyone else ever had, I guess we hadn't yet covered a few of the basics, like where my parents worked or which school he'd been kicked out of.

We'd get there. I wanted to be the keeper of his every detail, the world's foremost expert on everything about his life. I would catalog and index every fact of him, learn the pieces and moments that made up the whole, keep them safely archived in my heart. Just as he would keep mine.

Aiden yanked the car to the side of the road and shoved it into park. He grasped both my hands in his.

Confusion tottered through me. "What are you—"

"Promise you won't let them turn you against me." His voice was low and urgent, his eyes fierce with need.

"What? Never." I drew back from the intensity. His fingers gripped mine tighter. "Aiden, nothing they can say could . . . I know you. I love you." The words felt strange on my tongue. I wasn't used to saying it yet and I worried it sounded hollow, insufficient, even though I knew it was true. I said it again, more forcefully. "I love you. Nothing's going to change that."

He kissed me—hard at first, then softer, more trusting, almost teasing. Each touch of his lips was like the quiver of wings, a butterfly released into the air around us, until we were surrounded by them, the whole car filled with flutter and magic. I was high off his kisses, high off him. High on the knowledge I wouldn't let anything stop us.

"I love you too," he said, and my heart flooded over with happiness.

"Let's go to your place," I murmured as I kissed my way from the corner of his mouth, up his jawline, toward his earlobe.

He shook his head. "No. Let's go to Canalside."

I started to laugh but Aiden wasn't kidding. The rejection hit like a slap. "Really?"

He was already refastening his seat belt. "I told your parents I'd be taking you skating. I don't want you to have to lie to them tonight. Not because of me." He touched my lips, soothing the sting. "Believe me, I want you more than I've ever wanted anything. But we can wait a few more days. I promise I'll make it worth it." He tapped me on the nose and I smiled despite my disappointment. "Besides, it'll be fun."

"Okay," I said. "Let's skate."

SEVENTEEN

IT *WAS* FUN. MORE THAN FUN, ACTUALLY. ROMANTIC and cheesy and teen-movie perfect, right down to the poppy soundtrack and the tongue-searing cocoa.

I had been to the rink at Canalside a few times sophomore year with Jo and Eric and Eric's then-girlfriend, Jasmyn (sweet, upbeat, and miniature except the boobs: one hundred percent Eric's type), but going with Aiden was different. For one thing, he really knew how to skate. Circling the ice with Jo was always a bit terrifying—just when I'd start to find my balance, she would clutch my arm with a whoop and pull us both down, shrieking with laughter. Two minutes later, I would do the same to her. With Aiden's steady, patient hand in mine, I didn't have to worry about falling. I knew he would hold me up through anything.

Before we'd even laced up our skates, the scene with my parents felt far behind us. It had sucked but we'd gotten through it, just as we would get through whatever else life—or parents—threw our way. I wasn't worried. Even in that brief encounter,

Mom must have been able to see how much Aiden had changed. And if she hadn't, she would see it soon enough because this boy was in my life to stay.

At three minutes before ten, I turned my key in the front door and was greeted by Rufus's quick, eager sniffs and the happy swish of his tail. "Hi, Rooey Roo," I said. "Hi, good dog. Where's your duck?" He perked his ears, pounced on the duck toy that was slouched near the shoe rack, and trotted into the kitchen beside me. I was suddenly desperate for a tall glass of water. All that skating and talking and kissing had left me parched. I'd been too busy drinking in everything about Aiden to hydrate properly on the ice.

"JoJo?" Mom called from the living room, over the sounds of the television and the tap filling my glass.

"Yup," I called back. Damn, that water was delicious. Why had I never noticed how delicious water could be?

"Come in here and talk with us," she said.

I refilled my water, stepped just far enough into the living room to be technically present, and leaned against the door frame. Even parents couldn't pop my bubbling good mood, but that didn't mean I wanted to settle in for a long winter's chat.

Dad hit pause on their show. "How was the skating?"

The smile took over my face before I could stop it. "Fun. Really fun."

"Good. Did you eat?"

"Yup. Grilled cheese. Hot chocolate. Oh, and half a pickle." Aiden was right—it was nice I didn't have to lie about what we had done.

Dad quirked a grin and I remembered he sometimes almost had a sense of humor. "Sounds nutritious." I wondered what he'd been like before he met my mom.

Mom cleared her throat and gave him a pointed look. He set down the remote. "We're glad you had a nice night and got home safely and on time," he said. Mom nodded along. "But your mother and I discussed it and we're not comfortable with you hanging out with this guy."

My heart stopped. "You *what*?" Dad shifted in his seat, uncrossing and recrossing his legs. I didn't wait for him to continue. "That's not fair. You don't even know him."

"I do know him, much better than you do," Mom said. I opened my mouth to object, then shut it, realizing that as far as they knew I'd spent a grand total of about four hours in his presence. Disabusing them of that notion would not help my case. "And although I'm sure he's grown up a lot in the past three years, the Aiden I knew was a very troubled young man. He showed a lot of unchecked anger toward authority, especially women in authority, and had some highly destructive tendencies, toward himself and school property and others. It takes a lot to get expelled, you know." I didn't react. I was feeling a lot of anger toward authority myself, but it wouldn't help to show it. "I trust he was on his best behavior with you tonight, but he's not someone your father and I approve of you spending time with."

"But Mom—"

"It's not open to discussion. I'm sorry, JoJo. You'll have to find someone else to go out with."

"Find someone else?" I repeated. Could she even hear how ridiculous she sounded?

"Maybe Eric has a nice friend he can set you up with for prom," my dad said.

I gripped my water glass. This conversation was getting inaner and more insulting by the second. As much as I wanted to fight back, I knew the best thing I could do was let it end, stat. I'd be eighteen in five weeks, done with high school in fourteen. What were they going to do, lock me in a tower until graduation? Continue to micromanage every aspect of my existence until I was as old and unhappy as they were?

"I know we can't protect you from everything, but it's still our job as your parents to help you make good decisions. And getting mixed up with Aiden Jamison would not be a good decision," Mom said. Her voice sounded firm but I could hear, too, that she wasn't enjoying this.

I let my face go flat. "Whatever. I don't know if he was even going to ask me out again anyway."

She gave me a pitying little smile that made me want to explode. "If he does, feel free to blame your big, bad parents for why you have to say no. I'm sure he'll understand."

I steadied myself on the exhale. "Am I excused? Are we done here?"

She nodded. "Good night, sweetheart. I'm sorry."

I put my glass in the dishwasher, gave worried Rufus a pat of reassurance, and headed upstairs to bed. It was a disappointing end to an otherwise wonderful evening but, now that they'd had their say, I couldn't even muster up real anger about it. As I washed, brushed, and flossed through my nighttime routine, I just felt deflated. It was sad how my parents kept proving their irrelevance. Obviously I was not going to stop seeing Aiden. Obviously they couldn't do a damn thing about it. How annoying that we still had to go through these motions. But if they didn't want to have a real relationship with me, fine. We'd keep playing pretend until I was out of here for good, never to look back.

Their loss.

Jo texted, **How did it go?**

Ludicrously, I wrote. **They don't want to let me see him**

Ugh, she replied, and I could only shake my head. Not exactly the rush of sympathetic rage and support I might have expected from my best friend.

You okay? she asked.

Yeah, I responded. **Whatever. Tell you more tomorrow**

I'm sorry, Bee

I slid into bed and pulled the blankets up high, my whole body tense as I waited for the sheets to get warm. Fuck my mother, too, for always keeping the heat turned so low. It was a miracle I didn't wake up winter mornings with frostbite on my nose.

My phone buzzed and I groped for it on the nightstand. The screen lit up with a text from Aiden. **Good night beautiful. I love you**

The glow washed through me, pushing everything else out.

Sweet dreams, I wrote back. **I love you too**

I pictured his smile and let my hand slide back under the covers, down to the spot where I wished his hand would go. I imagined it was Aiden's fingers pressing against me in a slow, steady circle that got firmer and faster until all the day's stresses were released. Fuck what my parents thought. Nothing mattered but us.

EIGHTEEN

I WOKE UP SLOWLY, HALF IN DREAMLAND, HALF OUT, and blinked against the fog of morning consciousness. The house, my room, seemed somehow off, unfamiliar, in my still-sleepy blur. All was quiet, yet the light through my curtains already blared with the full force of the day. I rolled over to check the time through half-shut lids and my heart bolted at the jump-start: 9:37. *Shit.*

Of course the one time in the history of existence that my parents let me sleep in was a day I was due at work by ten and had not set an alarm. Because usually in this house an alarm was unnecessary.

Shit shit shit shit shit shit shit. I untangled myself out of bed and gave my armpits a quick sniff. There was no time for a shower but I definitely needed to take two minutes to soap off in the sink.

I stumbled into the bathroom, pulling my hair into a ponytail, gargled mouthwash while peeing, soaped my hands, face, and armpits, applied deodorant, brushed my teeth, and was done.

Today's customers at the Sugar Shack would have to be forgiving. This was as attractive as I could get in eight minutes or less.

I was too late to eat breakfast so I almost missed the note my mother had left on the kitchen counter: *Hope you slept well. Have fun at Jo's tonight. Please don't forget to get gas before you come home.*

I exhaled my annoyance. I never forgot to get gas. It was yet another rule that had been drilled into me: When you borrow the car, you must return it with a full tank. Probably the only reason my parents ever allowed me to drive was so they wouldn't have to stop at a gas station. I crumpled up the note and tossed it at the recycling bin. Perfect shot.

The gods of traffic and parking took mercy on my soul and I slipped through the employee entrance in the back and punched in at 10:04:49—late, but borderline acceptable.

"Joanna! You made it." Mr. Sugarman lifted his impressively bushy eyebrows toward the clock.

"Yes, I'm so sorry I'm late." I shoved on my visor, tied back the apron, and gave him my best ready-to-go face.

"Well, luckily the customers are a little late this morning too," he allowed. "We've got a new shipment of caramel corn and some milk-chocolate rabbits to stock. It looks like Easter is all about the milk chocolate this year. Nobody wants the white rabbits or the dark. You'd think they'd mix it up: pair a milk-chocolate rabbit with some dark chocolate eggs, but no. Milk, milk, milk, milk, or nothing."

"Hmm." I tried to look like I cared. "Maybe milk-chocolate

buyers are all early birds and the dark-chocolate people are more last-minute types." Easter was still several weeks away.

"Perhaps," Mr. Sugarman said. "Perhaps. We must be prepared either way." He lifted his fist. "Onward! The work of the day awaits us!"

We got to it. For the next few hours I hoisted, unpacked, and broke down boxes; bagged, weighed, and priced the caramel corn (while sampling several kernels to avoid passing out from hunger); swept, sprayed, and scrubbed all kinds of surfaces; rang up purchases, helped with flavor conundrums, and snuck in a few texts while Mr. Sugarman was in the back room or jollying it up with customers. Aiden was at work too—changing oil, fixing headlights, and replacing some lady's transmission—so his responses were short but sweet. Jo was either sleeping in or not near her phone because my **SOS no breakfast. Hurry, send falafel** message went unreturned. Jo never missed an opportunity to joke about falafel.

When Mr. Sugarman finally released me onto my lunch break, I scarfed down a sandwich and walked a few blocks to try to clear my head. My brain kept replaying last night's conversation with my parents, cycling through everything I wished I could have said to them. How insulting it was that they didn't trust my judgment. How infuriating that they wouldn't even engage in a real conversation about it, just decided what they thought should happen in my life and laid down the law. How delusional they were to think it was up to them.

The more I replayed it, the angrier I got. They hadn't even

bothered to pretend to respect my choices. And they had in no way given Aiden a chance.

Jo's theory about my mom was that she was even harsher with herself than she was with the rest of us, and that she felt so much pressure—as a woman and as a control freak—to do things the Right Way that she was unable to let down her guard, even a little bit, ever, so she was always one small push away from snapping. Jo felt mostly sorry for her, but Jo had the luxury of distance. I not only had to put up with my mom every day, I had to worry about her neuroses being echoed in me. My biggest fear was that I would end up just like her—and if she had her way, that's how it would be. No wonder she found Aiden so threatening. But I knew, I *knew* he was good for me.

I lifted my face to the sun, breathed deep, and tried to let it go. My parents could say whatever they wanted; I wouldn't let it affect my life. There was power in deciding *screw them*. But it was frustrating that I even had to.

I returned to the Shack to find Mr. Sugarman gone, Lexa scooping ice cream for a mom and her three already-bouncing-from-the-sugar kids, and a familiar figure lingering by the St. Paddy's Day candies: Eric. I went over. "May I help you, sir?"

He gestured toward the display. "I'm overwhelmed. Who knew there were so many different shamrock lollipops?"

I adjusted my visor. "So you need assistance choosing amongst the many kinds of suckers?"

He nodded emphatically. "Yes, please. Which one sucks the best?"

"I assure you they all suck," I said. "Deeply."

His dimple appeared and I felt a rush of satisfaction at making him crack. "But which one delivers the happiest ending?" he asked. The mom shot us a dirty look and ushered her kids toward the register. Lexa gave Eric a little frown. He mouthed *sorry* and we shared a conspiratorial grin. Eric's girlfriends never appreciated our sense of humor.

The customers left and Lexa pouted adorably while Eric gave her a quick kiss good-bye. I pulled out my phone. Finally, a text from Jo.

Gaaahhhhhh you won't believe what happened

What? The bells jingled as Eric pushed his way out the door. "Later, Betts," he called. I waved back to his salute.

I'll tell you when you get here. HURRY UP

I grinned at the screen. "Aiden?" Lexa guessed. She sighed. "You're so lucky."

I slid the phone into my apron pocket. "My parents want us to break up. They think he's 'trouble.'"

I dropped the air quotes and her eyes went Bambi wide. "But you guys are so perfect for each other. It's, like, *destiny*. You can just see it."

"You can?"

She nodded and I realized I was quite fond of her. "It's obvious. I saw it from the start. You guys have something really special."

"Yeah," I admitted. "We do." That seemed ungracious so I added, "But so do you and Eric, right?"

Her shrug was so small I almost missed it. "Eric's great but it's not the same."

Pride and curiosity battled for space inside me. "It isn't?"

"I mean, I love him, don't get me wrong. But it never feels like he's really mine. He's such an enigma." She paused. "To be honest, I used to be a little bit jealous of you and him."

"Of me and *Eric*?" That was shocking.

"Don't be mad. You just . . . you guys have always had this easy back-and-forth and you know each other so well. It's so clear in his face that he admires you and thinks you're really smart. He never looks at me that way."

I laughed. "He never looks at you like you're his pal and his sister's best friend because you're his *girlfriend* and he wants to make out with you. It is different. I'm just his friend."

She looked at the floor and I almost wanted to hug her. I'd never seen the fragile side of Lexa before. "He's such a good boyfriend but he doesn't really let me in close, you know?" I shook my head. I didn't know. Eric had never been like that with me. She looked up. "It's been six months and he's still never said 'I love you.' And we don't . . . we're not having sex. I want to but he doesn't, so we're waiting."

I tried to hide my surprise. "Waiting for what?"

She blushed. "Waiting for him to be more sure about me, I guess. I don't know. He says he isn't ready yet."

My jaw dropped to the floor. "Eric's a virgin?"

She busied herself with the retro candy bars, which did not need straightening. This conversation was unbelievable. I wished I had a witness. "I shouldn't have told you. Please don't tell Jo." But Jo probably already knew. "I just feel like he's been acting extra distant these days and I thought maybe you might know what was up."

"I'm sorry. I don't." A group of customers came in and Lexa gave them her sunniest smile. As I helped one person and the next, her observations about Aiden and me ping-ponged through my brain, ricocheting off my anger at my parents and my half-buried irritation with Jo. The fact that Lexa could see what was special about Aiden, while for some reason Jo refused, only added to the burn.

Antsyness skittered through me so I turned away from the couple that was entering and went to get my spray bottle and rag. I needed to clean. As the shift ticked by, my impatience with everything—Jo's distance, my parents' bullshit, this job, the world . . . everything that wasn't Aiden—multiplied until I was so worked up I could barely count change without seething.

There was only one solution: I needed to see him. Only being in his arms could make things seem right again.

I texted Jo, **Gotta stop by Aiden's first**, and powered off the phone as her **Uh . . . okay** flashed across the screen. I didn't need her judgments. Fifteen minutes later I was buzzing his doorbell, kissing the surprised smile off his lips, and letting him lead me by the hand, up the stairs, into his bed, where the rest of the universe melted away.

NINETEEN

SEX WAS BOTH EVERYTHING AND NOTHING LIKE WHAT I expected.

In the movies, it seemed pretty straightforward and obvious: The guy lies on top of the lady, thrusts his hips, and ta-da! They're fucking. But it turns out the parts don't just slide together on their own. The guy has to be kind of . . . positioned for entrance, and it took us a few tries to get it in right.

Once he was inside me, we were all systems go, though it slipped out a couple times and had to be put back in. *I am having sex,* I thought. *There is a penis inside me.* It was such a strange and surreal thing to be happening, I couldn't help grinning. The longer we kept at it, the more hilarious it seemed, and soon I was full-on giggling.

Aiden paused. "Is this okay?" he asked.

His expression was so serious, it made the giggles come harder. "Yeah. Sorry. It's just, don't you think it's funny? I mean, a funny thing to be doing?"

He frowned. "It doesn't hurt?"

I shook my head. Not exactly. It was strange and a little uncomfortable, but not painful. It had pinched at first, but then it felt good and kind of hilariously awkward, like some goofy but awesome new dance we were learning together.

But Aiden was not grinning or laughing. He propped himself up on his elbows and stared into my eyes and kind of stroked my face and hair while moving slowly in and out of me, until I giggle-snorted and he turned his head away. A few more thrusts and he laid his full weight on top of me and said, "Okay, I'm done." I stopped laughing.

I traced my fingers over his back and wondered if he'd come. Or had he given up or gone soft because I was laughing too much? I couldn't tell. I hoped I hadn't embarrassed him. He held on to the base of the condom and pulled out, rolling over to face the wall. I curled myself around him with one hand against his heart, and waited. Nothing.

I kissed the back of his neck. "Are you mad at me?"

He didn't move. "Why would I be mad?"

"I don't know. Because I was laughing and I thought maybe . . . Hey. I love you."

He nodded but didn't say it back. My stomach wobbled.

Just when I thought I might explode with confusion, he rolled over and covered my mouth with his. I kissed back, greedy for affirmation, and as we kissed and kissed and kissed and kissed, I felt him harden against my leg. He pulled off the old condom, flung it onto the floor, and, still kissing me, rolled on a new one.

He yanked my hips toward him and this time had no trouble getting himself inside. He pinned both my wrists and moved against me, much less gently than before. After a few seconds of pain, it felt good, physically. But it also felt like I was being punished.

He grunted and let out his breath with a full grimace, then collapsed onto the bed, spooning me close. He kissed my neck and squeezed my breasts and cuddled against me, all sweetness, and I wondered if I had imagined his anger.

"I love you," he said into my ear before kissing it, and whatever I might have done wrong, I felt forgiven.

TWENTY

WHEN I OPENED MY EYES, THE WORLD WAS PERFECT. I was lying on my side in Aiden's warm bed with his arm tucked around me, his body curled against mine. I felt the steady rhythm of his chest rising and falling and, without a thought, matched my breathing to his. My eyelids fell shut as we inhaled and exhaled together in sync, like two parts of one whole. I had never felt more complete.

We might not have been great at sleeping together yet—whatever, we would practice; it would be fun—but *sleeping* together was amazing. I was so glad I'd come here instead of going to Jo's. I never wanted to leave this moment.

My eyes flew back open. *Oh shit. Jo.*

I peeked at the clock on Aiden's dresser: 6:55 a.m. Too early to call her. Aiden had to be at work by eight, so his alarm would probably go off soon. Much as I wanted to stay nestled in his arms forever, I was suddenly all too aware I hadn't showered in two days or brushed my teeth since yesterday morning. Aiden might, as he'd said, want to know every piece of me, but I wasn't quite ready to inflict my morning breath on him. I slipped out from under his arm, hoping I wouldn't wake him, and walked quietly to the bathroom. My stomach grumbled a reminder that I hadn't fed it dinner.

I hadn't meant to fall asleep in Aiden's bed and stay the night, skipping dinner, bailing on Jo—but I also hadn't *not* meant to. Jo was probably livid. I didn't even want to turn on my phone and find out how pissed.

After we'd had sex that second time, Aiden had collapsed into sleep as I lay beside him, poking at the knot of my emotions. He'd snorted a few little piglet-like snores he probably would be embarrassed to know I'd heard, and I had turned my head to watch him sleeping. With his lips slightly open and his face relaxed in a dream, all his sweetness and vulnerability were right there on the surface. My heart surged with love as I thought of all he had trusted me with, and all I'd trusted of myself with him. I had tucked myself around him and vowed to never let go.

Jo would forgive me. Unlike me, she never stayed mad for long. And besides, she still owed me from the summer before fifth grade, when she forgot she'd invited me to go with her and Eric to the Erie County Fair, and I'd waited and waited for them to come pick me up and then cried all day while they ate cotton candy, caramel apples, frozen lemonade, and fried dough, and Eric threw it all up over the side of the Scrambler. I was still a little sad I'd missed that.

I brushed my teeth with my finger and swished the toothpaste around in my mouth, hoping it would cut through the scuzz on my tongue. I spit and rinsed and left the water on while peeing, to cover up the sound in case Aiden was awake. Not that he didn't know girls peed—but that didn't mean I wanted him to hear me doing it.

There were a few streaks of blood on the toilet paper when I wiped, and a slight soreness inside me that almost felt good, like I'd earned it. I knew having sex wasn't an achievement, but I couldn't help it—I felt proud, like I'd won a 5K or done a hundred pull-ups or something. Our first time may not have been fairy-tale perfect, but it was fun and real and romantic and ours. I wouldn't change a thing . . . except that one moment when Aiden had gotten distant, like he was angry at me or maybe just expecting more. I hoped I hadn't disappointed him. It was confusing how quickly his mood sometimes turned.

When I emerged from the bathroom, clean and wrapped in Aiden's red towel, the room smelled like coffee. Aiden stood in the kitchen in his underwear, hair messy and adorable with bed-head, pouring himself a cup. "Hey," he said.

"Hey." I felt oddly shy, given the things we had done to each other. But also, I wanted to do them again.

"Are you sure you have to go?" he asked. "You can't stay and be here waiting for me when I get back from work?" He was teasing but I was tempted. I loved that after a whole night together he still wanted me around. Even if we didn't talk or touch, just sat and stared into each other's eyes for hours or days at a time, I didn't think I could ever get sick of him.

He took a sip of coffee and held the mug out to me. I accepted it and he smiled and I knew that whatever came next—no matter how grouchy Jo was, or how annoying it would be having to hide him from my parents until I moved out for college and was finally free—it was worth the price for this happiness.

I blasted the radio all the way to Jo's place and let myself in using the hidden key. The house was quiet and still—only Stella seemed to be awake. She watched me coolly from her perch on the staircase and flicked her tail with judgment.

I removed my shoes, crept past her up to Jo's room, and shut the door gently behind myself. Jo was asleep, or pretending to be. I slid open a dresser drawer and helped myself to pajamas—the blue ones with yellow duckies. They reminded me of a game Kyle and I used to play when we were still young enough to take our baths together, a rubber-ducky adventure he'd inexplicably dubbed the Bubble-Pony Bing Bang. I'd loved that game. I wished I still remembered how to play it.

Pajamas on, I used Jo's lip balm to moisten my kiss-chapped lips, climbed under the covers, and slid into a dream of everything and nothing and *him*.

TWENTY-ONE

I SENSED JO'S DISPLEASURE BEFORE I SAW IT. IT WAS cast over me like a heavy woolen blanket, prickly on the skin, stiflingly thick, and scented with the tang of mothballs and irritation. I peeked at my best friend. She sat cross-legged on her side of the bed, watching me with a gaze like Stella's.

"Your mom called."

That woke me up. "When?"

"Last night. Around nine. She couldn't get through on your phone so she tried mine."

I waited, heart pounding. I'd never before been unsure whether Jo would betray me.

"I told her you'd passed out while we were watching a movie and did she want me to wake you up." Jo paused ominously and the air in my chest transformed to cement. "Lucky for you, she said no."

The cement crumbled. I resumed breathing. "What did she want?"

"She said she'd text but you're on your own for dinner tonight because they're going out with one of your dad's coworkers, so to please be home on time to walk Rufus and do your homework and lock yourself up in your cell like usual."

I met her eyes. There was no give in them. "Thank you."

She regarded me steadily. "You're welcome."

I sighed, wishing I could fast-forward through this part. We both knew how it would end. "Jo, I'm sorry, I fell asleep and—"

"And you didn't care that we had plans or that I was sitting around waiting for you all night, half wondering if you were dead, half furious that you weren't, because all you could think about was Aiden and you knew I'd get over it, so why even bother texting back to say you were standing me up?"

I swallowed. She was more pissed than I'd thought. And, snide comment about Aiden aside, she wasn't wrong. I should have texted her. "My phone's been off."

"Right. How convenient. An insurmountable obstacle."

I groaned and threw myself across her knee. "Please don't be mad. I'm the worst. I know I don't deserve you. Just . . . give me fifty lashes. With a noodle. Not a wet one. Beat me with a jagged, uncooked noodle until both I and the noodle doth break. Use *two* noodles. I beg you, show no mercy. Allow me to earn back my good name and your forgiveness."

I cast a hand across my forehead in my most beseeching swoon, and watched as she struggled to hold on to her anger. I could tell it was loosening, but the anger still won. "Betts. Just because you're in love doesn't mean you can be a total dick. I'm not your cover, I'm your best friend. Everything about last night sucked."

I felt a wash of shame. She was right.

"I mean you've known this guy for what, two weeks? And already he's more important to you than anything or anyone else? I get that he's hot but is it worth all this?"

I sat up. "All *what*," I said.

Jo gestured as if the *what* were in the air all around us. "Lying to your parents. Lying to me. Cutting work and ditching friends and giving zero shits about anything that isn't him. Dropping everything and everyone else to run to his side the minute he snaps his fingers and says *come*. Changing who you are just to fit some vision of what he wants you to be."

"Excuse me?"

"You've changed, Bee. I feel like you're slipping away from me and you don't even care." Before I could protest, she charged forward. "You have. The Betts I know wouldn't treat me like that. She wouldn't ditch me for some guy and force me to cover for her with everyone and make me stay up half the night wondering if she's ever going to bother to show. The Betts I know doesn't drink black coffee and only talk about her boyfriend and not give a shit when her best friend has something to tell her because all she thinks about is *him*."

I stared at a smudge on the wall by Jo's head and wished I could scrub it off. "I talk about things other than Aiden," I said.

Jo's eyebrow game was high. "Have you listened to us lately? We are failing the Bechdel-Wallace Test. All we talk about now is boys."

"We also talk about Sydney."

She didn't smile. "You are not helping your case."

I shrugged. If this was the way Jo felt—like Aiden was *some guy* and I was an awful friend because of one emergency mess-up and she couldn't support my falling in love because I wasn't going to be, as Tyson once put it, "Jo's little lapdog" anymore—then I shouldn't have bothered to come here. Considering my parents had just forbidden me from seeing the love of my life, my best friend could maybe be a little more understanding. I didn't need her to pile on about Aiden too.

"I'm sorry that my falling in love isn't intellectually stimulating enough for you. I'm sorry that the major thing going on in my life right now, the amazing and wonderful thing I want to be able to tell my best friend about, doesn't pass your big feminist test."

"That's not fair."

"Isn't it? Fucking Lexa is being a more supportive friend than you right now."

I expected her to fire back but instead her face got sad. "I just think that Aiden—"

"Stop," I cut her off. "You don't want us to talk about him anymore and I don't want to hear it." She looked away.

I picked some fuzz off my pajama top and studied the familiar pattern of Jo's comforter as we sat there in silence. I had already apologized for standing her up. I would not apologize for falling in love. If Jo couldn't accept that, there was nothing else I could do. Trying to force me to choose between them was not going to end the way she wanted.

After an eternity, Jo finally spoke. "Hey." Her voice cracked. "Don't cry."

"I'm not crying," I snapped, refusing to play into the joke. But when I looked at her face it was streaked with tears.

My anger broke. I lunged into the hug.

TWENTY-TWO

I STOOD BENEATH THE CASCADE OF MY SECOND shower of the day, letting my emotions unclench as the steam filled my lungs and the water hammered my back. Like everything else in Jo and Eric's house, the water pressure in their shower was perfect. I loved knowing I could stand there until every inch of my skin was puckered and prune-y, and still no one would bang on the door, reminding me not to waste water and that other people needed to be able to use the bathroom too, please. My mother enforced the five-minute shower rule as if the future of the planet depended on it. The Metmowlee-Rubens had three showers and no rules about any of them.

On the other side of the curtain, Jo tapped her toothbrush twice against the sink, a post-brushing tic I knew drove Eric nuts. "So do you want to hear the exciting thing that happened to me yesterday morning?"

The memory of her texts floated back to me through the steam. *Whoops.* I should have remembered to ask about that. "Of course," I said. "Tell me."

"Well. I was experimenting with glazes on a batch of cinnamon rolls—"

"Yum." Aside from the coffee I'd had at Aiden's, my stomach was still empty. I would have eaten six cinnamon rolls right there in the shower if only they were within reaching distance.

"Sorry," Jo said. "All gone. And, raisins."

"Oh." So she had already been mad at me, even before last night. Or maybe that was just what the recipe had called for. I reminded myself this wasn't about me. "Continue."

"So I took a few photos of how the glazes were turning out, and right after I post them, I get a message from Sydney saying, 'Those look delicious.'"

"A text?"

"A comment on my post."

"Okay." I tried to keep my voice encouraging but so far this story did not qualify as "exciting."

"So I was like, 'Come over and you can try some,' and she was like, 'Seriously?' and I said, 'I could actually really use a guinea pig,' and twenty minutes later she was sitting on a stool in my kitchen, *being my pig*."

"Wow," I said. Maybe I hadn't been giving Jo enough credit.

"I know. She stayed for, like, three hours, just chilling and talking and stuff. Betts, she is so amazing."

I could hear the big, dopey grin on Jo's face, even without seeing it. A snake of jealousy slid through me, the same hiss and tingle I used to feel if Jo got paired with someone else for an elementary-school art project or played too long with another kid on the swing set. I smiled it off. That was ridiculous. Sydney wasn't going to become Jo's new best friend. That wasn't the role Jo was going for.

"And Benji?" I asked, tipping my head back to rinse out the conditioner.

Jo paused. "Still on. We didn't talk about him much, really."

"Oh." I turned off the water and groped for the towel. When I stepped out from behind the shower curtain, her face was grim.

Shit. I hadn't meant to burst her bubble. At least, not entirely. I'd only wanted to deflate it a bit with a small prick of reality, to protect her from getting hurt too much down the line. But now I felt like an ass.

My brain grasped for something to distract her with. The news that Aiden and I had deflowered each other last night didn't seem like quite the right choice. "I saw Eric at the Shack yesterday," I volunteered instead.

Jo rummaged for her eyeliner. "So?"

"So," I said, bending over to wrap my hair in a second towel, "you were right, the other day. Something is up with him. At least according to Lexa." I flipped back up, adjusted my turban, and filled her in on what Lexa had said about Eric being distant and wanting to wait to have sex. If Jo was surprised on either count, she didn't show it. "Oh, and get this—she said before I met Aiden she used to feel jealous of Eric and me. Isn't that absurd? I mean, just picture me with Eric."

Jo drew a smoky line across her eyelid and flared it out into a wing. We'd gone through our learning-to-apply-makeup years experimenting right here in this bathroom together, but somehow she had become an artist while I had yet to demonstrate competence with even a wand of clear mascara. Luckily Aiden didn't like girls to wear makeup anyway. "It's not that absurd," she told the mirror.

I waited for the punch line. It didn't come. "It isn't?" I pushed.

She switched to the other eye. "I always thought you and Eric would be kind of good together."

"Seriously?" I half squeaked. I wouldn't have been more surprised if she'd said she wanted to date him herself.

"Yeah." She studied her reflection. "Actually, for a minute there I kind of wondered if when he broke up with Jasmyn, he might start something with you. I mean before he got with Stacy or Corina."

"And then Taylor."

"And Arum."

"And Monica."

"And Lexa."

"Don't forget Sonia Park," I said. She'd been the one before Lexa.

"Right." Jo grinned. "My Brother the Slut."

I steered clear of that one. It was one thing for Jo to semi-insult Eric, but another thing entirely for someone else to do it in front of her. She once stopped speaking to me for an entire recess because I had called Eric "booger brain" after he'd said *she* was a doo-doo head. It hadn't mattered one bit that I'd been defending her honor—putting down her twin was crossing the line.

"Don't get me wrong, it's not like I wanted you guys to get together," she said, tipping my world back onto its axis. "It's just, I could picture it working."

"I am so not Eric's type." But already the narrative was shifting in my head, and all those past moments of wishing and what-ifs seemed less pitiful, more bittersweet.

It didn't change anything about now, of course. He was still my friend and Jo's brother, and besides, I was in love with Aiden. But it was nice to imagine my secret crush had been slightly less pathetic than I'd thought.

Jo shrugged and put down the eyeliner. "Anyway. Clearly it doesn't matter now, but I'm sorry I didn't say anything about it back then. That would be weird, though, you know? My best friend and my brother?" She scrunched up her nose.

"Yeah. Totally weird," I said, mirroring her *ick* face. "And never going to happen."

She exhaled. "It feels good to confess. I hate keeping secrets from you. But it's like, saying it out loud might have made it come true, or something. Before. I didn't want to be a third wheel with my best friend and my brother. I need you both to always love me the most."

"Well, consider yourself forgiven." I'd always hated that math: If Jo was my favorite, and Eric was Jo's favorite, and Eric also loved Jo the most, then whose favorite was I?

But now it all added up to one easy answer: I was Aiden's and he was mine. There were no other variables or factors to consider. The equation was perfect, complete.

Bee + Aiden = Everything

TWENTY-THREE

SPRING FEVER HIT OUR SCHOOL AT FULL TILT, AN orgy of madness and hope, more frenzied than even in years before. My classmates were like wind-up toys that had been cranked slowly, all winter long, and were now finally released to their literal and metaphorical flips, spasms, and somersaults. The hallways and lunchroom were mayhem, and half the teachers seemed to give up on even trying to make us learn. We were seniors. That was fine with us.

I didn't know if my parents felt sorry for me after squashing my romantic prospects, or if, like everyone else I knew, they were distracted by the slight lift of winter's grays and forgot to be total dictators for a minute, but now that I had decided to ignore them and their rules, they were being uncharacteristically lenient. When I wasn't at school or working my shift, I was "studying with Jo" almost every waking moment of the next few weeks, and my parents barely said a peep. Of course, no real studying got done. Kissing, though: A lot of kissing got done.

Caffeinated walks by the river, chilly picnics in the park, and hot chocolate and games of Uno with Aiden's little brother and sister, who were even cuter in person than in their pictures, and adorably in love with him. Kendra was prone to misty tears over games she didn't win, and to fits if she thought you were letting her, but Aiden was a master at both sneakily playing to lose and turning her frowns into giggles. I loved being his coconspirator in it.

From everything I knew about Aiden's history with his mom, I'd kind of expected the whole family to be damaged by how she'd left them. But Alex and Kendra seemed like normal, happy kids, and their dad, though I rarely saw him, always offered an easy smile and a laid-back "Well, if it isn't the famous Bee." Maybe Kendra and Alex had been young enough when it happened that they weren't as affected as Aiden. Or maybe once Aiden cleaned up, he'd been able to help them adjust and get through it. He was an attentive big brother and it was clear just being near him made them feel safe and free—much how I felt on our long rides to nowhere, the motor humming through us, my arms wrapped around him, our hearts and bodies flying.

There was more sex happening, too. We were getting good at it, I thought. Most of our afternoons were spent naked in his apartment, exploring every inch of each other's skin, sharing every random thought in our heads. We were doing exactly that in the stolen extra hour after one of my shifts, when Aiden's kiss to my kneecap was punctuated by the sound of a car door closing in the driveway—his father returning home from work. I rolled onto my back. "Do you think your dad knows we're having sex?" I asked.

Aiden kissed his way up to my hip bone. "I doubt he thinks about it. But if he did I guess he'd probably assume yes."

"You don't think he cares at all?"

Aiden shrugged and continued the kiss trail across my belly, toward my ribs. "It's different with sons." I stiffened and he laughed. "Don't get mad. That's how the world is. I didn't say it should be, it just is." Perhaps he could sense my desire to rage against that, so he softened it with "My dad knows the way I feel about you. That's all I meant."

I accepted the diversion. "How do you feel about me?"

"I love you. You're my life."

The kisses moved up the side of my breast and approached my neck. "Yeah, but what do you like about me?" I asked.

He nuzzled under my chin. "Everything."

I rolled onto my side and wriggled lower so we were face-to-face. I'd been fishing before—for compliments, affirmation—but now I really wanted to know. I wanted to hear him say it. "No, I'm serious. That first day we met, what was it that made you want to make some big romantic gesture for a girl you'd only talked to for ten minutes in the candy shop?"

He shrugged. "I'm a romantic kind of guy."

I exhaled in frustration. "So it had nothing to do with me at all?"

"What? Of course not. Where is this coming from?"

I rolled away. I felt ridiculous, but I couldn't let it go. "I just want to know why me. Why you liked me. Why you love me."

"Bee." He touched my face but I didn't turn toward him. He moved closer and pressed his lips to my shoulder. "It's you.

I know you. And I love every wonderful and maddening thing about you."

I burrowed a little deeper into the pillow. "Like what?"

"Like how stubborn you are." He teased my shoulder with a bite. "Like how delicious your skin is. Like how fun it is to eat you up." I squirmed and his voice got serious. "It's not even a choice, Betts. You're part of me. It's like a reflex or an instinct or an eleventh toe, but way better than that sounds. And way more than that too." I forgave everything and rolled back toward him, but he kept talking. "I love the face you make when you're lost in thought, how you kind of bite your lower lip and blink in threes, and don't even know that you're doing it."

"I do?"

He blinked three times at me. "Yeah. I love the way you over-think everything but still try to act chill. How you have the biggest vocabulary in the world but also appreciate corny knock-knock jokes. I love your body and your brain and the way you move, the way you look at me. I love that you hold my heart in the palm of your hand and could crush it completely with the slight-est flinch, yet somehow you're the one who needs *me* to list all the reasons I need and adore you."

I lifted my neck to smash my lips against his and fell back into the pillow, knowing the kiss would follow me. My heart bubbled at the thrill of the things he'd just said. I didn't know if I really held that power, the power to crush him, but I felt a rush at hear-ing he thought so, a rush at being so needed.

"It's not some checklist or formula," he said. "It's *you*."

I believed it because I felt that way too.

* * *

The first crocuses pushed up through the frost-crusted ground and Mr. Sugarman scraped the shamrocks from the windows of the Sugar Shack, painting eggs and chicks and bunnies in their place. "Jesus sure died for a lot of pastels," Eric noted when he dropped by our shift to see Lexa. I grabbed my spray bottle and got busy on some imaginary smudges, to give them the illusion of privacy. But Eric followed.

"Killer Bee, what's up with my sister? She's been moping like a wilted daisy all weekend."

"She has?" I asked. She'd seemed fine that week at school, at least as far as I had noticed.

"Yeah. I thought maybe you guys had some kind of fight."

I shook my head. I hadn't seen a whole lot of Jo outside school, since I'd mostly been hanging with Aiden, but as far as I knew, we were good. We had been careful with each other ever since our big fight. I could tell she was trying to be more supportive about Aiden, and I tried to talk about other things. Last week she had learned she'd gotten into Brown, her top-choice college, and I had hugged her and cheered and not even re-googled the 405.7 miles between the Geneseo campus and Providence, Rhode Island. Her mood probably had something to do with her unrequited yearning for Sydney, which had gotten nowhere in the past few weeks, but if Jo hadn't told Eric about that herself, I certainly wasn't going to. I made a mental note to check in with her later and pushed away the guilt that I hadn't done so already. If Jo needed me, she had my number. I couldn't be expected to magically know if something was up.

Eric leaned against the ice cream case. "So you haven't been avoiding us?"

"Nope." It was half true. I hadn't been avoiding Jo at all.

Eric, on the other hand, I'd been keeping my distance from. Ever since Lexa and Jo had made it seem not so outrageous that there once could have been something between us, I had felt extra aware of that *something*, whatever it was or wasn't, whenever Eric was near me. I hoped taking a step back from him would allow the feeling to pass.

Besides, I'd been busy with Aiden. There wasn't time for much else.

"Good, because that would be tragic," Eric said. He looked over at Lexa but she was helping a customer, so he wiggled his fingers in her direction and headed for the door. "Don't be a stranger now, you hear?" he called to me as he backed out of the Shack, nearly slamming into Aiden.

"Sorry, man," Eric said as he stepped out of the way. Aiden nodded sharply and walked inside.

"Hey!" I slid my arms around his neck and felt the happiness spread to the tips of my ears. "You got off early."

"I thought I'd surprise you." He looked over his shoulder at where Eric had been. "Who was that?"

"Eric. Jo's brother."

Aiden frowned. "Was he hitting on you? It looked like you were flirting."

"No!" I swallowed. Had I been? "No way," I assured us both.

He stared like he didn't believe me. "He's Lexa's boyfriend," I explained, gesturing over at her. Lexa looked up from the register where she was ringing up three cellophane-wrapped Easter baskets, and gave Aiden a cheerful wave. His shoulders dropped.

"Well, as long as he knows you're mine."

"He does," I promised. "And I am."

He kissed me. "Good."

I nestled against him and resolved to be more careful.

"Hey," he said, shifting his weight, and only then did I realize he'd been keeping one hand behind his back. He held out a bouquet of orange and yellow tulips, and grinned at my surprise. "Happy six-week anniversary. I love you."

No one had ever given me flowers before, aside from the three-dollar school-fundraiser carnations Jo, Eric, and I exchanged on Valentine's Day, attached to the grossest haikus we could think of. This year Jo's card to me said, *Circumstances change but my underwear doesn't. So crusty. Such goo.* Eric had written, *This morning I pooped and thought of you as always, hoping you pooped too.* I treasured that tradition but this was far more romantic.

I accepted the stems of sunshine and spring and looked into his eyes. "I love you too."

TWENTY-FOUR

"I'm sorry you were down but I love it when you bake off your problems," I said around a mouthful of rosemary shortbread with tart lemon glaze. "Mmph. These are like buttered sunshine in a pine-tree forest. But way tastier than that sounds."

Jo smiled more to herself than at me. "Eric's perception of reality is not always to be believed. But thanks. Things are definitely looking up."

"Good." I didn't push for details. She clearly was enjoying acting mysterious. She hadn't been very forthcoming on the phone last night either, and then Aiden had called so I'd switched over to him and it had gotten too late to call her back. But whatever she may or may not have been moody about, she seemed to be over it now.

We stopped at my locker and I snuck a glance at my screen while sliding my Latin book onto the top shelf. I typed a quick reply to Aiden's text. Jo looked away.

"So, what do you want to do for your birthday?" she asked as we wove our way toward the lunchroom. "You're staying over Friday, yes?"

"I'm not sure," I hedged. "I have to check with Aiden."

"We could all hang together. Invite him over."

"Yeah, maybe." But I knew full well that we wouldn't.

Jo shot me a look of the *don't do this* variety. She was onto me.

"He might be thinking more like dinner just the two of us," I confessed.

Her jaw muscles twitched and I steeled myself for a fight. We always celebrated our birthdays together, even the year she and Eric had chicken pox. But she exhaled through her nose and said only, "Okay. It's your birthday. You should get to do what you want."

I hated this new politesse between us, the don't-ask-don't-tell tiptoeing around the Aiden-shaped elephant in the room. Our conversations had morphed into an overly timid boxing match, all bobbing and weaving and circling around the point. Every now and then Jo would send out a light jab—an "Oh, well if *Aiden* thinks so" when I'd mention his opinion, or a "Wow, he's even worse than your mom" when he'd text to find out what I was doing—but for the most part, she behaved, and when she was snide about him, I ignored it. These were the rules of our unspoken truce. There was no good solution for this problem between us, the problem of him, so we stayed normal on the outside and avoided the conflict within. In moments like this I found myself waiting for the bubble to burst, both wanting and dreading it.

But I wasn't about to throw the first punch. It was easier to let things be and keep dancing around it.

"Betts! Jo!"

I winced out of pure habit but, for once in her life, Cicily had excellent timing. She and one of her spirit-squad minions— Sheila? Shira? I could never remember that girl's name—squeezed in between us. "Did you get your tickets for spring formal yet?" Cicily asked, slightly breathless. "It's three bucks cheaper in advance than if you buy them at the door."

"Good to know." Jo caught my eye and we were united by our shared understanding of the universe and Cicily's role within it.

"The decorating committee's planning some really cool stuff." Shelby/Sheena sounded almost accusatory—maybe Jo and I weren't being as subtle as we thought.

Cicily turned to me. "Are you bringing Aiden?"

For a second I could see it: the teen-movie version of my life. Hair upswept, heels low. Smile shy. Dress long. The boutonniere on Aiden's blazer and matching corsage on my wrist. His eyes bright in the dim lighting as he led me to the dance floor and pulled me in close. We'd slow-dance even to the fast songs, oblivious to the world around us—our private bubble impenetrable even by the sloshing fruit punch of the jocks bouncing beside us, the chaperones' bored-but-watchful glares, the flashes from photos being snapped and posted where my parents might find them. . . .

Nope. It could never happen. Not that Aiden would be into it anyway. He would surely deem it "too high school."

"I don't think we're going," I told Cicily.

"Uh, yes we are," Jo said.

I shook my head. "I can't bring Aiden to that." Cicily's eyes sparked with interest. I imagined a crow pecking them out.

"So what? You'll go with me." Jo pulled out her wallet. "Two, please," she said, and I clamped my mouth shut until the transaction was over, to avoid further feeding the gossip troll.

We stepped into the lunchroom, and Cicily and Shana scampered away. "Since when are you all gung-ho about spring formal?" I asked. We hadn't gone since freshman year.

Jo looked at me sternly. "It's the end of our senior year. We've got this and maybe prom and that's it—we'll never go to another stupid high school dance again." She waved a ticket in my face. I took it. *Normal on the outside.* It was easier not to fight it.

"Happy early birthday," she said. "Prepare to dance like everyone's watching."

TWENTY-FIVE

THE INSTANT THE INTERCOM SOUNDED OUR RELEASE, I flipped my history notebook shut and bolted from my desk, ready to leave the school day far behind. This week already seemed endless and it was still only Monday.

Jo smirked at me from her desk, two rows behind mine. "You're like Pavlov's dog," she said as she stood.

"Meaning?"

"The final bell rings and you immediately start salivating, like, *Aiden time!*" She stretched her arms above her head and a peek of midriff appeared. I reached out and poked it.

"Would you prefer to linger here a while longer?" I offered. But I wasn't mad. She was right. I was walking out of the classroom and down the hall with Jo, but my heart and mind were already in his arms.

When I got to the parking lot, Aiden was waiting. "Can we go to the lake?" I said instead of hello. "I want coffee and fresh air and to leave this place forever."

He delivered a kiss along with my helmet. "Your wish is my command."

Soon the caffeine was coursing through me, pushing the antsyness out my pores, as we walked with our backs to the wind and our fingers laced together. "Alex taught me a new one last night," he said.

"Oh yeah? Let's hear it."

"Knock, knock."

"Who's there?"

"Etch."

"Etch who?" I asked and nodded, anticipating the punch line.

"Gesundheit," he supplied. His smile was bashful. "Alex delivers it better." But I loved that he saved up goofy jokes for me.

We stopped to watch a cluster of ducklings—so fuzzy and awkward, they must have been freshly hatched—as they tumbled into the water and after their mother, who sailed straight ahead without looking back. One veered inches from the group, thrown off course by a wave, and peeped frantically as it kicked and flapped its way back into line where it belonged. I wanted to laugh but I could feel how intently Aiden was watching them, and it shifted something inside me. He took everything so seriously, my Aiden, even those silly little ducks. I had never known anyone like him.

His hand caressed my side and I turned to kiss him. He tasted like coffee and springtime and him-ness. Delicious. "What's this?" he asked, pulling the dance ticket from my pocket.

I explained about Jo, the formal, and Cicily's lunchtime

ambush with Shelly or Sheri or Shirlee. Aiden frowned at the slip of paper, and my stomach sank with the feeling I had done something wrong. "So you're going without me?" he said.

I looked up in surprise. "You want to go to a high school dance?"

"No," he admitted. "But I'd prefer if you weren't trying to hide it from me."

My mouth dropped open involuntarily, before the words sputtered out of me. "I wasn't hiding it. This only happened a few hours ago and I really didn't think you'd want to go."

"Well, I don't want you going with somebody else."

I laughed. "I'm going with *Jo*."

His face pinched tight. "Sure, and there won't be other guys there. Just a big empty dance floor for you and your lesbian friend."

I held still as the truth spread through me, cold, brittle, and sharp. "You don't trust me," I said. It wasn't a question.

He shrugged.

Panic crashed through the ice that had formed in my veins and replaced it with hot desperation. I grabbed his hand. "Aiden," I pleaded.

He pulled away. "I trust you," he said. "But that doesn't mean I trust every guy who comes near you. And you haven't exactly been—" He threw his hands up, tossing whatever it was into the air, unsaid.

"What? I haven't been what?" I felt as frantic and off course as that little lost duckling, but I tried to keep my body calm.

"Never mind." He looked away.

"No, tell me. Please. Whatever it is, I want to hear it," I said, even though my lungs were thick with fear. Aiden's sullenness was like a brick wall dropped between us, but I would do whatever it took to smash through it and get back to him. Whatever I'd done wrong, I needed to set it right.

His sigh was part exasperation, part defeat. "Honest with me. You haven't exactly been honest with me." I stared at him with total incomprehension. "There wasn't any blood," he said.

I shook my head, still not getting it.

"On the sheets. When we had sex the first time. It's okay you weren't a virgin; I just wish you'd told me the truth."

My head swirled with confusion. I heard the accusation but had no idea how to process it, or how to prove it wrong. "I *was* a virgin." It rang hollow even in my own ears. "Aiden, you were my first."

He grimaced. "Forget it. It doesn't matter."

"I'm serious," I said. "And I did bleed. Not all over the sheets, but after, when I was wiping. There was blood on the . . ." My cheeks were hot with shame, even though I knew I hadn't done anything wrong. Why didn't he believe me? "I use tampons, and I've—" I stopped short of describing how Tyson's fingers had once slid inside me. I'd never regretted any of the things I'd done with my ex, even though I regretted some of the ways he'd treated me, but for the first time, I wished we hadn't. "I swear I've never slept with anyone else."

"Okay, I believe you," he said. "Let's forget it."

The lump of defeat felt heavy in my throat. I swallowed hard and wished I could pull Aiden back to me.

"I would love to go to the dance with you," I tried. "I just worry that my parents—"

Aiden yanked his arm back so suddenly and so fast, my muscles seized in a wince, certain he was going to hit me. Instead, his half-full coffee cup hurtled past my ear and slammed into a tree trunk, exploding like the shock and fear inside me.

"Fuck your parents. No, seriously, fuck them. Are we going to hide from them forever? Is that your plan? You're going to keep me a secret for the rest of our lives? Or until you get sick of me and move on?"

"No," I whispered, held frozen by his anger, like a deer in the headlights of an accelerating semi—frightened and mesmerized, both. I'd had no idea he was upset about this. If I'd known, I never would have mentioned it.

"Are you ashamed of me? Is that it?" I shook my head but he wasn't waiting for an answer. "They don't own you," he said. "You're almost eighteen years old. Let me talk to them. Let them see how good we are together. And if they don't like it, screw them. You'll pack up your stuff and move in with me. We don't have to sneak around like this. They can't stop us."

"You want me to move in with you?" I felt three steps behind.

"Yeah." Aiden took my hand. "My dad won't mind—my family loves you." I'd still only talked to Aiden's father a few times in passing, but that was as irrelevant as how many card games I'd played with Kendra and Alex, or how often they took turns braiding my hair. This had nothing to do with his family or mine. It wasn't even about us. My hesitations had to do with *me*.

I'd pictured myself staying at his apartment semi-regularly on weekends, once college had started and I was officially on my own. I'd even imagined us living there together next summer, two coffee mugs in the drying rack, my stack of books nestled beside his. But it was impossible to think of us doing that now. "I can't," I said.

"Why not?"

"I'm in high school."

"So what?" He walked backward, pulling me with him, his face almost giddy now. "You'll still graduate. Then we'll get married and I'll follow you to college, or you'll defer for a while and figure out how to transfer here." He cupped my face, his touch gentle. "I want to be with you. I'll move the world to make it happen. You don't have to decide now, just promise me you'll think about it."

He smiled in a way that made me want to say yes to everything, though I wasn't even sure what he'd asked, or that any of it was what I wanted. Aiden was my future; I was certain of that. But I wasn't ready to upend everything else I had planned. I wasn't ready to get married or give up Geneseo. I didn't want to be a freshman living off-campus with a husband. That idea seemed preposterous. But since I loved him, why not? What was my problem? I did want to make him happy, and I knew he would do anything for me.

It was too much too soon, but even thinking that felt disloyal.

I closed my eyes and let him kiss away my confusion. The storm had blown over, but I still felt the wreckage from the winds.

TWENTY-SIX

MY PHONE BUZZED FRIDAY MORNING, TWO MINUTES before the alarm, with a wakeup text from Aiden. **Happy birthday babe. I love you**

Babe. I'd always hated when Ty called me that. It felt so generic, like I was one in a series of interchangeable girlfriends, not even worth assigning my own pet name to. Which I guess in Tyson's case had been true. Even at our most involved, I'd been incidental to him. He hadn't been central in my life, either.

Aiden, of course, was the opposite. He had made me his everything, right from the start. I loved that. I wanted that. But ever since Monday afternoon at the lake, I felt the weight of it in a different way. For a moment, just a flash, that *babe* felt almost suffocating. I shook it off. **I love you too. Can't wait to see you**

I flopped against my pillow and stared at the ceiling, still stickered with the burst of five glow-in-the-dark stars I had begged to affix there when I was six because my brother was getting constellations on his ceiling and I'd wanted to be just like him.

I was eighteen years old. It was the first day of my adult life and I was lying in a twin bed, gazing at the faded, peeling remnants of my childhood. Time to get up.

My phone buzzed again. **You look like a monkey and you smell like one too. Total coincidence that it's also your birthday**

Speaking of my brother. **What are you doing up so early?** I typed back. It was 5:32 a.m. in Chicago, where he'd escaped to on full scholarship. **Don't college kids sleep until noon?**

Haven't gone to bed yet. Don't tell Mom

God, I couldn't wait for that freedom to be mine.

Check your email. I sent you some tunes for getting older to. And tell Rufus happy birthday from me too

☺ **Will do**

Rooey and I technically did not share a birthday—he was a shelter dog who'd been picked up as a stray, so we didn't know when he was born—but when I went downstairs for breakfast he had a giant floppy ribbon tied to his collar, just like the one he had worn when we'd gotten him eight years before.

"There she is," Dad said, looking up from his hand-brain. He put down the phone and lit a candle he'd stuck in the top of a blueberry muffin. "I'll spare you the singing." He shook out the match.

I moved around the counter to hug him. "Thanks, Dad."

Mom bustled in as I blew out the flame. "Happy birthday." She kissed my cheek as she breezed past, toward the almost-whistling teakettle. "Half day today, right?" She eyed the clock on the microwave and reached for her travel mug. "Better open your present and move fast or you'll miss it."

I took a seat on the kitchen stool beside Dad's and pinched a bite from the muffin. Not as tasty as Jo's baking but not bad for store-bought. Beside my plate was a white box with a blue gift bow and an envelope on top. Dad had written on the envelope, *With great power comes great responsibility. We trust you'll use it wisely. Happy 18th birthday. Love, Mom and Dad.* I tore open the flap and unfolded the paper inside. It was a voter registration form.

"Haha. Thanks," I said. Dad looked exceptionally pleased with himself.

I stuck the gift bow to my forehead and lifted the top off the box. My parents had stopped using wrapping paper on presents around the time I'd stopped believing in Santa—i.e., when Kyle had discovered the truth at school and promptly ruined it for me, too. "We kept the receipt so you can exchange it," Mom said as I pulled down the zipper on the navy, white, and gray Geneseo hoodie and pushed my arms through the sleeves. It was cozy, soft, and just the slightest bit oversize.

"It's perfect," I said. "Thank you."

"You're welcome." Mom picked up her purse and headed toward her coat. "Have a good day. Put your plate in the dishwasher before you go, please."

"But what should I do with my juice glass?" I muttered while the front door closed behind her.

My father shot me a warning look. "That's enough."

I would never be an adult in my parents' house.

When I got to school, Jo did not spare me the singing. She met me at the entrance and delivered a full-blown serenade on the walk to my locker, which she had draped with purple streamers and stuffed with yellow balloons. I pulled out the balloons and tapped them into the air, one by one, watching them bounce and float their way down the hall from one kid to the next in a spontaneous game of Keep It Up. One ricocheted off OJ, who stomped away in a cloud of annoyance. "Sorry," I called after her.

"It's your birthday? Happy birthday!" Cicily squealed, coming up behind me and attacking with a hug. "That's so special that it falls on Good Friday and Easter weekend."

"Um, yeah." Easter this Sunday meant a day off from the Sugar Shack, but since I'd be spending it riding in the car with my parents and eating hard-boiled eggs and canned pineapple at my grandparents' house, while deflecting Gran's encouragements to "at least try a little bite" of the ham, I would maybe rather be at work. But at least today's early dismissal meant I could see Aiden as soon as he finished his shift, and I'd have time for a birthday milkshake and fries with Jo at the diner in between.

Or so I thought. But when the final bell rang at twelve thirty, releasing us into the world, we stepped into the bright sun of the afternoon, arm in arm, and seconds later, the world went dark.

"Hey!" I yelped, swatting at the cloth that had been dropped over my eyes, but my assailant was already securing the blindfold in place.

"Happy birthday, Bumble Bee," Eric said as he took my other arm. "I am pleased to inform you that you are being kidnapped." Jo whooped and they stepped forward, pulling me with them.

"Haha, very funny, you guys." I tried to yank my arms free.

"Nope, no struggling," Jo said. "Only cooperative prisoners get their arms back."

"Is this really necessary?" We lurched in what I assumed to be the direction of the senior lot. If I looked straight down, I could see a narrow strip of ground at my feet, but it hurt my eyes and didn't really tell me much.

"No, but isn't it fun?" she crowed. There was nothing I could do but go along with it.

"Halt!" Eric jolted us to a stop and dropped my arm. I heard the jingle of keys and the click of the Wildebeest unlocking. "Watch her head."

Jo slipped my bag off my shoulders and guided me into the car with her hand on top of my skull, like cops do to handcuffed perps on TV. Even though I'd been climbing in and out of cars my entire life, it was surprisingly difficult to do so blindfolded. "Birthday girls get shotgun," she said. She leaned across me to fasten the seat belt. "And no peeking."

The door clanked shut beside me. I heard the click of Eric's seat belt, and the Wildebeest purred to life. Music shot out through the speakers and he quickly turned it down. I realized I couldn't remember the last time I'd sat in this car, which I used to catch a ride in most days of the week. Strange. "It's nice of you to play chauffeur for Jo's schemes," I said.

Outside the car, Jo laughed and shouted, "No, a polynomial ring! But with unicorns!" at someone across the parking lot. I wondered if it was Sydney.

"Actually, this was my idea," Eric said.

"Oh." I settled back in my seat. Usually Jo took the front and I leaned forward from the backseat to hear them over the music. It was kind of cozy up here. "Where are we going?"

I felt Eric smile. "If I told you, what would be the point of the blindfold?"

The passenger door opened and shut behind me, and Jo cried, "Let's go!" She put her hands on my shoulders and I felt her bopping to the music as Eric backed us out of the parking space and accelerated toward whatever was next. "I know you don't love surprises, Betts, but you're gonna like this one."

"As long as I'm back by two fifteen."

"Nope, no can do," she said. I tensed. "Relax, I just texted him—from your phone, which I am confiscating for the remainder of this outing." My heart raced with panic and I tried to protest, but Jo talked over me. "We'll drop you off at his place by six. And I already asked your mom if you could spend the night at our house, so what you *should* be saying is, 'Thank you, Jo, you are the best,' because now you can hump all night like birthday bunnies and no one will be the wiser."

My neck warmed with a blush. I hadn't actually told Jo that Aiden and I were sleeping together, but of course it wasn't hard for her to guess. "Aiden's okay with it?" I asked, hating how that sounded but still needing to check. I hoped Jo had made clear to him that this was all her doing, not mine. Things had gone back to normal after our first fight, or whatever that was at the lake on Monday—he'd been tender and attentive, and hadn't mentioned marriage or my parents or my hymen again—but I was still feeling cautious, like I had something to prove, and I didn't want to risk giving him any reason to be mad. It would be one thing if I could have told him about the change of plans myself, but Jo could be an uncouth messenger.

"Aiden will be fine. If he had a problem with you hanging with your very bestest friends, what kind of boyfriend would he be?" Jo said. Great, so it was going to be that kind of day with her. Of course Jo had no clue that real relationships involve compromise.

"Be nice," Eric said. "It's her birthday."

"Sorry," she allowed. I wondered how much they'd discussed us and what exactly they had said.

"So how come he doesn't ever hang out with us?" Eric asked, as if it would be normal for Aiden to catch rides in the Wildebeest or sit around in their kitchen eating scones. Eric's girlfriends were almost never included in that stuff, and all of them were still in high school, not older like Aiden.

"Jo hates him." That wasn't entirely fair, but if Jo could be flippant about it, so could I.

"I don't hate him! I barely know him. I hate that I never see you anymore."

Maybe it was the blindfold or the plain honesty in Jo's voice, or the way I'd always felt safe and loved inside this car, but the sadness that flooded the back of my throat, pushing hard against my eyeballs and catching me by surprise, drowned all the fight in me. I suddenly needed her to be able to see in Aiden what I did, to understand how it felt to be loved by someone the way he loved me. "He's a good person," I said, but of course the words were inadequate. I wished I could beam the feelings straight into her brain instead.

Her hands returned to my shoulders and squeezed. "I don't think he's a bad person, Betts. I'm just not sure he's a great person for you."

Jabs of defensiveness pricked at my spine but I breathed in and tried to match Jo's calm. It was bizarre, having this conversation in a moving car with a cloth over my eyes, Jo's words floating behind me, Eric silent and steady by my side. But the surreality also made it safer to ask, "In what way?"

She paused. "Do you really want to know?"

"No," I admitted. An eternity ticked past. "Okay, yes. Just tell me."

"He seems kind of . . ." I waited while Jo chose her words. "Don't hate me, but: needy. In a way that makes him kind of controlling. And a little possessive."

I stared into the darkness of the blindfold and saw the coffee cup exploding against the tree trunk and the flash of his anger, sudden and startling and directed at me. *No.* I shook my head. "It's not like that. I promise." Jo didn't react but I could feel her not believing me. "If anything, *I'm* the needy one."

"I hope I'm wrong," she said. "I really do. And I'm wildly jealous of every second he gets to spend with you, and therefore totally biased. But also, I miss you. I miss my best friend."

"You see me almost every day."

"You know what I mean." Her voice was so sad and serious, I almost couldn't take it.

I did know what she meant, though. And in that moment, I missed her too. I missed how we used to be.

Maybe Aiden would be willing to try again, to go out with us someplace fun and low-key and in neutral territory. Then she'd see that he was sweet and good, and good for me, and understand why I loved him more than I'd ever loved anyone besides her. Maybe I didn't have to keep my two worlds separate.

Eric shifted in his seat, unclicking his seat belt and mine, and I realized the music had stopped and the car wasn't moving—we must have parked. Before I could do anything, Jo lunged to take my hand. "Listen. You are this weird, wonderful, flawed, perfect, beautiful, ridiculous, uptight, amazing human being, and I am not going to allow time or distance or anyone with or without a penis to stop you from being in my life forever. Okay?"

I rolled my eyes even though she couldn't see them. That was perfectly Jo: over-the-top dramatic. "Okay," I said.

"Good."

Eric cleared his throat. "Well, on that note . . ." He pulled off my blindfold and I blinked at the sudden brightness. "Surprise!"

TWENTY-SEVEN

I LAUGHED. AFTER ALL THAT FUSS, WE'D ENDED UP AT Bob's Diner, half a mile down the road from where we'd started.

Jo bounced out of the car. "Did we fool you?"

"Yes. Very clever."

She and Eric beamed twin smiles, as proud as the ones in the photo of them with a giant sandcastle they built when they were four. "We had lots of ideas of other places to take you, but we decided that classic is best," he said.

"Besides, this is our place," Jo added.

I hooked my arms through theirs. "It is."

The scent of griddle grease and deep-fried everything assaulted our nostrils as we pushed through the front door and headed for our usual booth. I slid in across from Eric and hitched over for Jo, who plopped down beside me. "Hunnnngryyyy," she moaned, leaning into me. The woman Eric had dubbed the White Waitress approached (lots of the servers at Bob's were white, but this one was almost translucent), and Jo sat up and waved away the plastic menus. "We'll take three chocolate milkshakes and three orders of fries, please." She turned to me. "Our treat, of course."

"Well, thanks." Unlike Jo, who loved her own birthday, I usually found the yearly attention a little embarrassing. But this was exactly the right level of fuss.

I unwrapped the silverware bundle the White Waitress had dropped in front of me and polished my spoon with the paper napkin, while Eric described the horrific eating habits of some of the kids he'd coached at youth soccer camp last summer, and Jo started a round of Would You Rather: The Disgusting Things to Eat Edition. A feeling of pure contentment spread through me. Before I had met Aiden, this was hands-down my favorite place in the world to be: together with Jo and Eric, anywhere. The past few weeks of senior-year weirdness, I'd worried things had already changed irreparably. The relief that they had not was almost euphoric.

"Enjoy," the waitress said, walking away from the feast she'd delivered. Jo produced a candle out of nowhere and stuck it into my fries.

Eric flicked a lighter into the wick and met my eyes over the flame. "Happy birthday, Betts."

I closed my eyes, and a wish formed behind my lids—that wherever our separate paths might take us, we would always find a way to return to this kind of togetherness—then opened them, leaned forward, and blew.

A wisp of smoke coiled upward and Jo cheered like I had blown out two hundred candles instead of one. I salted my fries, dragged one through the milkshake, and popped it into my mouth. Perfection.

"Sooooooo. Did you hear about Sydney and Benji?" Jo paused, eyebrows raised, to make sure she had our full attention. "They broke up this morning."

I had not heard that, but I *had* seen Benji hitting on Bekah Parsons outside my English class, so I guessed this explained that. "He dumped her a week before the formal? What a dick."

"No, she broke up with him."

I grabbed another fry. "Oh. Carry on, then."

"Wait," Eric said, "how is that fine? Guys can be heartbroken too, you know."

"It's fine because now she's free to go to the formal with *me*," Jo said.

Eric tipped his head to one side. "With you?" I watched as he processed that. "Oh. Huh." He nodded like it all made sense, which of course, fundamentally, it did. "Cool." Jo's expression shifted from challenging to pleased, and I wanted to hug him for having reacted exactly perfectly. "So it's a date-date?" he asked.

"I hope so."

"You already asked her?" I said.

"Not yet, but I've been laying the groundwork. Wooing her by baking, like you suggested."

Eric's face betrayed the same mix of caution and protectiveness I was feeling too. He spoke gently. "I don't know if she's into . . . I mean, do you know if she's ever kissed a girl?"

"No." Jo was unfazed. "But neither have I." Eric and I looked at each other and he gave the slightest shrug. Jo pulled a big sip through her straw and leaned back against the booth. "Look, guys, calm down. Sydney probably isn't bi or gay or pansexual or whatever, but so what? I'm not asking her to marry me; it's just a stupid high school dance. If she says no, she says no. So you can stop teaming up with your *Oh dear, poor Jo* glances. I've got this. But thank you. Your joint concern is truly heartwarming. A-plus."

I scooped up a spoonful of milkshake and wondered if Aiden had tried to reach me. I knew there'd be no retrieving my phone from Jo's grasp, but I really, really hoped he was okay with this. It could ruin our whole evening if he didn't believe I hadn't known what Jo was planning. "So I guess this means you're ditching me."

Guilt flashed across her face. "Is that okay?" I was surprised to discover I was almost disappointed, though not disappointed enough to get in the way of Jo's plan.

"You're not taking Aiden?" Eric asked. I shook my head. "So let's all go together. As a group. Us three and Lexa and Syd, once she says yes."

"Cool," Jo agreed.

I hesitated. "Lexa won't mind?" I was pretty certain Lexa would mind. The group date might make Aiden feel better about my going, though. And I had to admit, it did sound like fun.

He shrugged and stole a fry from the edge of my plate. "I'll ask but I'm sure she'll be cool with it." I nudged the fries a few inches in his direction. He had already polished off his own.

Jo stood. "I gotta whiz. Don't even think about touching my food, Eric."

"Like I'd want your cooties," he said.

"We used to share lollipops when we were little," she called over her shoulder, and Eric stuck out his tongue like he always did whenever Jo brought up this "fact."

He dipped three of my fries in Jo's milkshake and we shared a grin as we chewed. He leaned forward. "I know Jo's been giving you shit about Aiden, but I wanted to say, I'm glad for you."

I swallowed. "You are?"

"Yeah. If you're happy and he's good to you, that's great. You deserve that."

"Thanks." It was strange of Eric to say it, but surprisingly nice to hear.

"She'll come around. She's always wary of my girlfriends at first too."

That was an understatement. "I've noticed."

The right side of his mouth quirked up in the almost-grin I always thought of as Eric's secret weapon—made all the more effective because of his obliviousness to its power. I'd seen everyone from teachers to toddlers to, especially, teenage girls fold helplessly before it. I liked to imagine myself among the immune but of course I was no exception. "Senior year is weird, isn't it?" he mused. "I'm gonna miss you next year."

"You are?" I said for the second time, too aware I was sounding like I had a three-word vocabulary.

He looked surprised. "Yeah, of course. We both are."

Oh. "Same. I'm going to miss you guys too," I said, meaning it. Eric would be playing soccer and studying electrical and computer engineering at Cornell, which was less than two hours' drive from Geneseo, but of course we wouldn't be getting together without Jo.

Something shifted in his face and he looked at me so intently, I almost looked away. "Bee, I—"

He stopped, and in the corner of my vision, Jo reappeared, wiping her hands on her skirt. I guessed the bathroom was out of paper towels again. We watched in silence as she approached. "Sorry, guys, I should have said, you're allowed to talk to each other while I'm gone as long as you don't say anything too interesting," she said.

Eric rolled his eyes. "Now she tells us."

Jo slid back into the booth. "When's the last time you peed here?" she asked me.

I tried to remember. "No idea. Maybe February?"

"So you haven't seen the new mirror above the sink."

"Nope."

"Well. It's basically angled to ensure that you *have* to watch yourself go. This might be TMI, but it turns out my pee face is amazing."

I shook my head. "*TM* is exactly the level of *I* we want from you, always."

Jo snuggled against me. "I love you."

I cuddled back. "I love you too."

TWENTY-EIGHT

I BARELY HAD A CHANCE TO KNOCK ON THE DOOR
before Aiden pulled it open. "You're late," he said.

I hustled inside as though being quick now could make up for
it, and saw the microwave clock glowing 6:08. *Shit.* "Sorry. Jo
took away my phone and—"

He cut me off with a kiss. "It's okay. Happy birthday."
I relaxed. Of course he wasn't mad about eight minutes. Jo's
silly accusations had made me unfairly paranoid. He tugged
off my jacket and stepped aside, and I took in the scene before
me. Picnic blanket. Tea lights. Takeout containers. A single
red rose in a jar. The taut trepidation in my chest gave way to
happy flutters.

"This looks amazing."

"Are you hungry?"

"Starving." I was still kind of stuffed from the milkshake and
fries, plus the brown-sugar cupcakes with salted caramel frosting Jo had brought out after, but I knew that wasn't the answer

Aiden wanted to hear. He'd planned this whole romantic dinner for us. The least I could do was eat it.

"Kendra made me promise I would give you this *right away*." He held out a yellow construction-paper card that said *HOPPY BIRTHDAY BEE* in green marker across the front, surrounded by squiggles and colorful whirls. I opened it and an origami frog fell into my palm. There was a pretty good drawing of a tree frog inside, with *Love, Kendra P.S. Happy birthday too* underneath. I looked up, amused. Aiden's grin was full of pride.

"Please tell her I love it," I said.

He kissed my nose. "I will."

We sat on the blanket and I snapped apart my chopsticks while Aiden opened the containers of sesame chicken, fried rice, and vegetable lo mein—my favorites. Shadows and warmth from the flickering candles danced across his skin as he told me about a customer who'd caused a scene at the garage, and a hunch he'd had about an alternator bearing, which solved a problem that had been baffling his boss. His face was beautiful and animated, and I felt a shimmer of luck as I watched him talk. We'd been together almost two months but it was still sometimes hard to believe this boy was really mine. This—being in love, being with him—more than anything else about turning eighteen, made me feel truly, officially adult.

Aiden frowned. "You don't like it."

His displeasure snapped me out of my own head. I had only been half listening. "Don't like what?"

"The food. You're barely eating it."

"Oh." I shoved the tangle of noodles that had been lingering on my chopsticks into my mouth and chewed. "No, it's delicious. I was just focusing on what you were saying, and wondering if I'd even be able to pick an alternator out of a lineup."

The tension dropped from his shoulders. "You'd figure it out. I'm always bragging to the guys about how smart you are."

"You are?" I loved knowing he talked about me like that at work.

"Yeah. My little brainiac." He gave me a sticky sesame kiss. I chased it down with another mouthful of noodles. "Tell me about your day," he said.

"Mmph." I wiped the sauce from my chin and launched into it, from breakfast with my parents and the bow on Rufus's collar to the balloons in my locker and my kidnapping on the school steps. When I got to post-diner cupcakes in the Wildebeest, and Eric's and my cheeks smeared with frosting due to a sneak attack from Jo right when we were laughing too hard to retaliate, Aiden's face shifted, betraying his indifference. "I guess you had to be there," I said.

He tipped back his water glass. I stared at the pattern on the picnic blanket. I was boring him.

"I wish you had been. Maybe we could all hang out together sometime soon. You've barely met Eric and you didn't see the best side of Jo. You guys started on the wrong foot, I think."

He sighed. "I'm not really interested in hanging out with your friends."

His tone said I should drop it but I didn't. "Why not?"

He shrugged. "I just don't see what they have to do with you and me."

"They're important to me. You're important to me. I want them to get to know you." I hated how high my voice sounded when I got defensive. I hated spending my birthday dinner *being* defensive.

"Fine. You want us to spend our time together eating french fries and talking about homework and flipping through yearbooks with your high school friends? If that's really what's most important to you, I guess we can do that."

I looked down at my chopsticks. "That's not what I meant."

Aiden took the plate from my hands, set it on the blanket, and pulled me toward him. "C'mere." He kissed me and the bad feelings started to sink away, or at least swim less close to the surface. "I made you something."

"You did? What is it?"

The kisses moved down my neck. "Are you sure you want it?" he said, voice suggestive. He squeezed my hip.

I pushed him away. His innuendo was making me feel cheap. "Yes, please."

"Close your eyes."

I did as I was told. He held my hand, warm in his, and after a few seconds of rustling, slid something cool and solid onto my ring finger. "Is that—" I opened my eyes. A thin band of hammered silver glinted in the candlelight.

"Happy birthday."

I gaped at it. "You made this?"

"Yeah, at the shop."

A ring. He'd made me a ring. My chest vibrated with questions I didn't quite want to ask. But he'd put it on my right hand, not the left, and he hadn't, like, proposed or anything. It was just a ring. A beautiful, thoughtful ring.

I held out my hand to admire it. Even the fit was perfect. "It's amazing. Thank you."

"You like it?"

"I love it." I shifted closer and thanked him with my kiss. He kissed back and I instantly felt it—the two of us clicking right back into sync. Sometimes my insecurities and worries caused misunderstandings, or words fell short of expressing what we felt. But our bodies understood each other perfectly. This was a language we both spoke fluently.

Aiden flicked and teased his tongue against mine and I responded as his hands roamed the peaks and valleys of my body's terrain. He tugged at the neckline of my shirt and moved his lips to the skin above my collarbone, sucking lightly at first, then harder. I laughed and squirmed away. "You're going to give me a hickey."

"So?" he said, moving back in.

I tried to nudge him off me, but he would not be deterred. "So I'll have to wear a turtleneck all week."

"Good," he said between kisses. "Then no one else will be tempted by your delicious skin." He sucked again, hard.

"Aiden . . . No, stop." The ring I could tell my parents I had bought for myself, or pretend was a gift from Jo, but a hickey would be much harder to explain. I wanted him to want me, but I didn't quite want this.

He lowered me onto the blanket and pinned me down with his hands and lips. "I want everyone to see it and know that you're mine."

I kissed back, relenting a little. "Everyone already knows I'm yours."

"Yeah?"

"Yeah."

"Good." He hovered above me with a mischievous smile, then pounced. I shrieked as he flipped me over, pushed my shirt up, and sucked hard on my back.

"Aiden!"

"What?" He laughed and moved toward my neck again.

I rolled over and gave in.

TWENTY-NINE

GOOGLING "HOW TO GET RID OF A HICKEY" RETURNED more than 436,000 search results, none of them the insta-cure I was hoping for. I ignored all the hickeys on my back, stomach, and thighs—those weren't going to be visible to anyone who hadn't caused them—and focused on treating the seven red marks along my neck and collarbone, and the five on my wrist and arms. I applied hot and cold compresses—a microwaved washcloth, ice cubes wrapped in a dish towel, a frozen spoon—brushed them with a stiff-bristled toothbrush, scraped them with a penny, massaged in peppermint toothpaste, applied aloe vera hand cream, and pressed them with rubbing alcohol and the inside of a banana peel. After all that, they maybe looked slightly better, but honestly it was difficult to tell. They certainly weren't gone. I wore a high-necked sweater throughout the weekend, despite the sauna-like temperature at my grandparents' house. I did not try the ham.

By Monday the hickeys had morphed from angry reds to

greenish-purples, like an array of strangely placed bruises. I wrapped them as best I could with a scarf—the high-necked sweater was too ripe to be worn another day—and hoped no one would be looking too closely. With any luck, they would be distracted by the dark circles under my eyes. I had stayed up half the night messaging Aiden and half-assing a paper on a book I hadn't actually read, and I was almost too tired to care about anything.

I lumbered through the halls, a zombie in search of a sugar rush. Why didn't they have caffeine dispensers in schools? I fantasized about walking into the teachers' lounge and pouring myself a cup of coffee, but even in this desperate state, I was still a rule-follower at heart. The caffeine wasn't worth detention or expulsion. I dragged myself to the vending machine, stared at the choices, and cursed the school board for banning pop.

Jo bounced over. "Guess what guess what guess what guess what?" She didn't wait for me to respond. "She said yes!"

"Who?"

Jo swatted my arm like I'd been acting confused just to tease her, but my brain really was that tired. It caught up the millisecond before she cried, "Sydney!"

Of course. Wow. I put both hands up for a double high five. "Amazing. Hooray!"

She gave me the play-by-play of asking while I dug in my pockets for change. I fed my quarters and a nickel into the machine. Damn—twenty cents short.

"Here." Jo added two dimes and I hit the white grape juice button. "Don't forget to subtract two bucks from your app," she said.

For my sixteenth birthday, Dad had given me an app that tracked expenses and earnings, and charted them by category and subcategory, down to the last penny. It was weirdly addictive—and stunning to see how much I spent on root beer before Aiden introduced me to the joys of coffee.

The can clanked and thudded out of the machine. "A dollar eighty, actually. Twenty cents of that was yours," I said. She grinned.

I used the edge of my scarf to wipe the top of the juice can clean before popping it open. I tipped back my head and took a long swig, waiting for the fructose to hit. Instead, I got a brain freeze. Too cold. I rubbed the pain at the base of my skull and grimaced.

"What's that?" Jo was staring at my chest.

I looked down. No spills. "What?"

She nudged my scarf aside and touched a cluster of hickeys at my clavicle. "That."

I smiled a little. "It's from Aiden."

Her whole body went rigid. "Oh my god. He *hit* you?"

"No! They're hickeys. Calm down." She narrowed her eyes and examined them closer. I stepped back. "I promise," I said.

"Did it hurt?"

"No."

"Well, it looks awful."

I rolled my eyes and took another sip of the juice. "Thanks."

"I take it your parents didn't see those."

I shook my head. "I'm still alive, aren't I?"

"Fair point."

"I just hope they'll have faded by Saturday so I won't have to wear a Snuggie to the dance."

"They will," she said with all the confidence I'd hoped to find on the internet but hadn't. At the mention of the dance she was beaming again. "Are you borrowing my blue dress?"

"Yes, please." I would be the best-dressed fifth wheel around, but I didn't mind. Whatever sadness I had about not being able to bring Aiden was eclipsed by my gladness for Jo and her maybe-a-real-date, maybe-not, but-so-what plans with Sydney. It didn't sound like intentions had been made totally clear in the asking or the response, but the ambiguity didn't seem to bother Jo in the least. She had gotten the girl. She was practically doing cartwheels.

Her initial glee expanded into a giddiness that escalated to elation as she became increasingly hyper throughout the week. When she intercepted me at the juice machine again before last period on Thursday, her smile was so huge it was probably visible from space.

"I got it!" she crowed. She danced around, holding something up in front of my face, but it wasn't until she added, "I am officially licensed to drive" that my confusion cleared and I finally caught on.

"Congratulations!" I hugged her. I had completely forgotten she was retaking her driver's test—that explained where she'd been during lunch. I hoped my face hadn't shown it. "My little girl's all growed up."

She jingled the keys in her other hand. "Let's go for a ride after school."

Shit. I would not be winning any Best Friend of the Year awards, but I already had plans with Aiden. "I can't. I'm sorry."

"Oh, come on. Just a quick spin. Your parents will never know."

I hesitated. He'd been kind of moody and distant the past few days, as if his happiness and Jo's were inversely proportional. We were just planning to hang out at his place for a couple hours while I got some much-needed studying done, but still. He wouldn't like it if I canceled. We'd already gotten into sort of an argument last night, with him pushing me to give up Geneseo and stay here, and getting pouty and kind of belligerent when I admitted I really wanted to go. It was one of the highest-ranked colleges in the whole SUNY system, and I loved its ivy-and-brick campus so much it was the only place I'd applied. But it was true there were plenty of schools closer to home, and I could probably get part of my deposit back. Maybe he was right and I was being selfish.

Annoyance flashed in Jo's eyes. "Don't tell me Aiden can't spare you for one measly hour so we can—"

"No, it's—" I couldn't tell the truth or blame it on my parents' rules; she already had her fighting face on. "I have a dentist appointment," I lied, pushing away the guilt. "My dad's coming to get me, like, right after school."

"I thought that was tomorrow."

It was. "It got moved."

"Damn." She shrugged it off. "Well, you'll get to witness my mad driving skills on Saturday, so don't cry."

I shook the empty juice can over my head. Two small drops splashed onto my cheek. "I'm not crying, I just spilled grape juice on my face."

Jo laughed appreciatively. "You dork."

I wiped my cheek clean with my sleeve.

THIRTY

I TEXTED AIDEN TO COME LATE SO JO WOULDN'T SEE him pick me up after school, and lingered at the end of Calculus to keep from encountering her in the hallway. It sucked to sneak around behind my best friend's back, but at least I was avoiding pissing anyone off.

It was surprisingly nice out, the kind of summery spring day that made it hard to remember what winter had even felt like. I sat on a bench by the parking lot with my book and pushed up my sleeves to let the sun warm my skin. The hickeys were nearly faded now, just yellowish patches with a few red dots you had to look closely to see, except for the big one still purple on my back.

"You need a ride?"

I looked up from my book to see Tyson standing above me. He shifted, blocking the sun, and I tugged down my sleeves, just in case. "No thanks. I've got one."

"Cool." He plopped down as if he had every right to share my bench. "How've you been?"

I leaned away almost involuntarily, but relaxed when I heard the familiar rumble of Ralph approaching. I gave Ty my sweetest smile. "Great! Way too busy for small talk. See you around." I stood, gathered my stuff, and turned to give Aiden an extra-long kiss. We soared off without a glance in Ty's direction, and my heart sang a little song of victory all the way to Aiden's apartment.

I put down my bag and Aiden closed the door behind us. "Who was that black guy? Is he the reason you stayed late?" he asked.

"Tyson? No, he just happened to come over right before you showed up." I stretched my arms toward the ceiling, releasing a kink in my back. "Isn't it gorgeous out? Maybe we should take our books outside."

Aiden hung up his jacket. "You guys sure looked friendly."

I swallowed. He must have seen the way I'd smiled at Ty. Of course it had looked like flirting. Maybe it *had* been flirting. I couldn't believe I'd been so stupid, especially after yesterday's fight. I fiddled with the ring on my finger, my new nervous tic. "He's my ex. Very ex. Believe me, there's nothing left between us."

He frowned. "I don't like the way he was looking at you."

My pulse quickened. "I promise I want nothing to do with him. I'll never talk to him again if you don't want me to."

"Did you sleep with him?"

"No! I told you, no." I stepped toward him, my head swarming with regret. "Forget him; he's nothing. Please."

His eyes narrowed. "Is he going to be at your little dance on Saturday?"

I threw my hands up. This was ridiculous. "Who cares?"

He reached out suddenly and gripped me by the arms. My heart jolted as he gave my body a shake. "*I* care. Why the fuck can't you see that?"

"Aiden, stop. You're hurting me." It felt like his fingers might press right through my flesh. They dug in farther as he shook me again. My biceps burned and my knees began to buckle.

"Not nearly as badly as you're hurting me." He shoved me away, fast and hard, knocking me off balance.

I stumbled backward and fell against the counter. My head throbbed on impact, but I was almost too startled to register it as pain. I blinked, seeing nothing but my own shock, and only realized I was on the floor when Aiden rushed over to crouch by my side.

"Bee, baby. My Bee." His voice was as stunned as my heart. He pulled me into his arms and kissed my face gently, murmuring my name over and over as his cheeks grew wet with tears. Whether he was crying from the scare of watching my fall or the emotional overload that had caused it, I couldn't tell. I barely understood what had happened, couldn't trust my own mind to determine what was real. I couldn't comprehend being a girl whose boyfriend would knock her to the ground on purpose. The rage I'd seen in his face and felt in his grip didn't match the story of *us* in my brain, didn't fit with the tears he was crying. The Aiden I knew wouldn't do that. He couldn't. Yet here I was, on the cold tile floor, aching inside and out. "You know I would never hurt you," he said. "I love you so much."

I love you, my heart echoed. *I love you.*

I felt his hand on my back, warm and tender, rubbing calm, soothing circles into my skin.

The clouds in my brain dissipated, and guilt seeped in as he cradled me against him and soothed and pleaded. The words settled over me, a blanket, a salve.

"I'm sorry," he said. "I'm so sorry. You fell. It was awful. You're okay. I'm so sorry."

I let my body melt against him, felt the love pouring out of his embrace. But I felt something else now too. His desperate fear of losing me. My own sudden fear of what he'd proven he could do.

That's not what happened. That's not what happened, my brain pulsed with each twinge. But which truth I was disputing, I didn't even know.

I tasted tears in the back of my throat—metallic, sharp—before I felt them press at my eyes. My head throbbed. My chest burned. I tried to remember to take in real breaths.

"It's okay," I said, "I'm okay," hoping the words would calm us both. I knew he needed to hear it, and I wanted to believe it was true.

THIRTY-ONE

ALONE IN MY ROOM THAT NIGHT, I UNZIPPED MY hoodie, pulled the long-sleeve shirt off over my head, and faced the mirror. Five purple florets bloomed on each bicep, reminders implanted by Aiden's fingertips. I pressed the marks with my own fingers—they were tender, but I almost welcomed the pain. It pulled me out of the relentless buzzing in my brain, the mix of shock and adrenaline that had taken over my system, and gave me something tangible to focus on. Nothing made sense, but when I pressed those bruises, I knew: These marks were real. This pain was real. Aiden had really done this to me.

I let go and felt confused and intoxicated.

I slept hard through the night and when I awoke, the high was gone. My body felt heavy. Drained. Sticky with the residue of an emotional hangover. Examining the bruises in the light of day, I barely recognized my skin or myself. They no longer hurt, but the rest of me—my insides and ego, my stomach and heart—ached through and through. Unanswerable questions and deep sadness swirled and pooled with the humiliation rising up in my throat like bile. How could I have let this happen to us. How could we have gotten to this place. How was I going to hide the marks from Jo?

I groped for the distraction of my phone and saw the middle-of-the-night text I had slept through. **I love you so much.** He'd repeated it dozens of times yesterday, until the words lost their meaning and became something else, a burden I couldn't reject. An obligation to say and feel it too.

I *did* feel it too. I loved Aiden. But what did love even mean if it could push us to a place like this?

I clicked off the screen.

I should tell someone. My parents, Jo. But I knew I wouldn't. I couldn't stand for them to think they'd been right about him.

They weren't right. They didn't know us.

I wished, suddenly, deliriously, that I could tell Eric what had happened. Eric, who, unlike Jo, would listen without judgment. Who would be calm and reassuring, irrevocably on my side. Who wouldn't blame me for being the person I was now.

Of course I couldn't tell Eric. I couldn't tell anyone. But I *could* make sure this never happened to us again. I would love Aiden better, be more careful not to hurt him, so he'd never again be pushed to hurt me in return. That much was the least I could do.

I love you too, I typed back, and willed my fingers to stop shaking.

* * *

I pulled myself together enough to go through the motions of a regular Friday, which meant, in effect, that's what it was. By paying real attention in my classes, indulging Krystal's obsession with Rasputin and the Romanov dynasty at lunch, giving Eric a high five each time we passed in the hallway, and joking around with Jo like everything was normal, normal, normal, I managed to stay focused on the present and avoid thinking about anything else. Nobody seemed to notice that my surface was bruised and my insides were crumbling. Nobody except Rufus, who that morning had leaned his full weight against my legs, placed his head on my lap, and stared up at me soulfully through breakfast, even though he knew he wasn't allowed in that part of the kitchen. But my parents had both left early for work, so there was no one to yell at either of us about any of it.

Even getting around my lie about the dentist turned out to be easy, since when my dad came to pick me up for my appointment, Jo was already in the library doing peer tutoring for our school's community service requirement. But as I sat across from the receptionist's desk, tuning out the world and the waiting room chatter, all the feelings I'd been keeping so firmly sealed out began to leak in past my defenses. They flooded the infinitesimal cracks in my resolve and streamed into the back of my throat, forcing me to swallow hard against them.

I grabbed a parenting magazine from the stack on the table in front of me and flipped through it slowly, trying not to think about the hundreds of other fingers that had touched its pages or what else they'd touched before that, but my brain could only block out one terrible thing at a time. I fled to the bathroom to wash my hands with soap, in water turned as hot as it would go. When I emerged, I felt calmer. I made it through the mandatory small-talk with the hygienist, settled back against the dental chair, closed my eyes, opened wide, and gave myself over to her control.

I knew it was weird to like going to the dentist, but every six months I looked forward to my turn in that chair. It was one of the few places in the world where I felt like I was doing everything right. The dentist always praised my obsessive flossing and good tooth genetics, and getting scraped clean and polished up gave me a feeling of accomplishment without having to do a single thing.

Jo and Eric once laughed at me for weeks because I'd called the dentist "my happy place," but I felt safe there. I felt worthy. And I always left feeling better, improved.

Today was no exception. As soon as the hygienist touched her silver hook to my gum line and started scraping off the plaque, everything I had been clenching so tightly relaxed and unspooled within me. It felt like she was chipping away not only at the buildup on my teeth, but also at all the confusion, guilt, and worry that had piled up inside me. A few tears escaped my eyes, rolling straight for my ears, and the hygienist paused her work. "You okay, hon?" I gave a slight nod and the scraping resumed. It felt good. I cried and she cleaned, and by the time my teeth were finished, I felt cleansed, inside and out.

It all seemed simple and clear now. I loved Aiden. Aiden loved me. Those were the two facts that mattered, but I'd gotten selfish and lost sight of that. Instead of proving he could trust me I had given him too many reasons to worry—it was no wonder he'd gotten so frustrated with me yesterday. But that was behind us now. We had gotten through it and we would move forward, stronger and better than before. We had to. I loved him. He was my world.

I called Aiden's phone while I waited outside for my dad to pick me up. It rang twice and went to voice mail. "Hey, it's me. I just wanted to hear your voice, but I guess you're busy, so here's my voice, telling you that I love you."

I hung up and focused on a clump of daffodils near my feet. It was springtime. The world was beautiful. Everything was going to be just fine.

The phone vibrated in my hand. **You are the most wonderful girl in the world**

I smiled. **Why thank you**

Climb out your window and run away with me tonight

I was pretty sure he was kidding. My window was on the second floor and I was liable to break my leg just thinking about jumping. **Okay. Where will we go?**

Everywhere. Nowhere. Who cares, as long as I'm with you?

I'd like to see the ocean, I wrote.

Yes. I love you so damn much. I'll call you later

I waved to my dad as he pulled into the parking lot. **I'll pack my swimsuit**

Better yet, don't

THIRTY-TWO

MOM'S RANDOMLY IMPOSED, STRICTLY ENFORCED
Family Nights occasionally approximated something resembling fun back when Kyle was still around, but ever since he'd abandoned me for college, they were so predictably torturous for everyone involved, I could only blame Mom's sadomasochistic streak for her insistence that they continue. I hoped that for this one she would let us pick out a movie to stare at together in silence, but when Dad and I arrived home from the dentist, the board games were already stacked on the table. Even my love of Scrabble couldn't make time tick faster, nor keep my mood from deflating like a punctured balloon. *Pop.*

Mandatory Quality Time was also phone free, just to further torture Dad and me. When I powered on my cell, it buzzed right away with a message from Jo. I held on to it, waiting for something from Aiden, but the longer I stood there, willing it to appear, the more fully I understood that nothing was coming. My stomach sank and my anxiety spiked to peak levels. It was the smallest of signals, more like the absence of one, really, but by this point I didn't need him to broadcast what he was thinking—I was hyper-attuned to each shift in his mood and heard it loud and clear. His temper was like my dog whistle. I wished I could plug my ears.

This was exhausting. It was exhausting and demeaning and, what felt worse was, I should have known. After all those apologies, after the flurry of kisses and promises and tears, after I'd handed back the power by letting him put what he'd done behind us and keep my heart, now this. He was pouting again, or giving me a lesson in who-knows-what. Maybe I'd taken too long to forgive him and now that I had, he was punishing me for the wait. Maybe he felt slighted that when he'd called twenty minutes after the dentist, I'd sent it to voice mail and texted **In the car with Dad**, and hadn't been out of my parents' sight since. Maybe he was jealous of the dentist and hygienist, or of my parents, or even my dog, because of the time I was spending with them.

I didn't know what I had done, but I knew it was my job to reach out and apologize now, to plead and try to prove whatever it was he needed me to prove. But I was tired. No matter how hard or how well I jumped through his hoops or ran when he called or rolled over at his command, it seemed it would never be enough. I'd been performing all day at school and performing for my parents all night, and I couldn't muster enough energy to jump for Aiden now, too. I was bruised and fatigued and just so over it, over everything. All I could do was text Jo back, get ready for bed, and sleep all my feelings away.

But my dreams were thick with panic. All night I ran in desperate search of things I couldn't reach, see, or find. I was helpless and inept and everyone in the world was mad at me—my parents, Jo, Aiden, even OJ. I had disappointed them all. It was as draining and overwhelming as being awake. I was sorry, so sorry, though I didn't even know for what.

In the morning, there was a text. **I miss you**

My defensiveness melted. I thought back to last night and almost laughed out loud at how paranoid and ridiculous I'd been, letting my insecurities and fears spin out and take over. Of course he wasn't giving me the silent treatment, punishing me for doing nothing. He'd just known I was busy, and was probably busy with family stuff himself. I'd gotten too wrapped up in my own head and let exhaustion take over, lost sight of all reason. I couldn't let myself freak out like that over what had happened on Thursday—it was an accident, and it was behind us. This was Aiden. He loved me. I needed to trust him and stay rational, remember he loved me.

I miss you too, I responded.

Skip the dance and hang with me tonight instead

My heart tugged in two directions. Much as I wanted to give in and say yes, to spend the night in his arms, letting him show and reassure me that everything between us was fine, I also really wanted to dance. I wanted a night with no drama, out with my friends, together like old times for what would probably be one of the last times. I wished Aiden could understand that, even more than I wished he could be part of it too.

I can't. I'm sorry. Jo would kill me if I bailed

Seriously? he wrote.

It's just one night. I'll make it up to you

You better

I read the words twice but couldn't tell if they were angry or playful. That was the problem with texting, it could be hard to interpret tone. But if I wanted to stop being anxious and mistrustful of every possible thought in his head, I needed to relax and stop second-guessing us.

Come visit me at the Shack today? I asked.

Maybe. Gotta go

I stared at the screen. Regret flowed through my veins. It made me feel helpless, the way he ran all hot and cold. I wanted to call him immediately and make sure we were okay. But I knew he was likely just busy at work, and I didn't want to seem too desperate and pathetic, even though that's exactly what I was, exactly what he'd made me. Exactly what I'd made myself, too.

All I could do was type, **Okay. I love you** and hope those words were enough.

THIRTY-THREE

SPRING SUNSHINE AND WARMTH BROUGHT THE CUS-
tomers rolling in at a steady clip through my afternoon shift. By
the time the hands on the lollipop clock ticked past three—the
hour Aiden got off work—I'd scooped so many ice cream cones
my arm muscles felt like rocks suspended in jello. A little flare of
hope ignited in my chest each time the bells jingled to signal an
incoming sugar-seeker, but after two hours of jerking my head
toward the door only to see it wasn't him, again, it finally sank
in: He wasn't coming.

He hadn't promised he would, but he also hadn't said he
wouldn't, or bothered to text anything else at all, and I couldn't
help feeling like I was being punished for choosing Jo and the
dance over him. I wiped my hands on my apron, pulled the ice
cream scoop out of its water-and-gobs-of-cream-froth bath, and
wondered if I should give in and go to his place after my shift.
I could text Jo and tell her that something had come up, maybe
place the blame on my parents. But no matter how good a lie I

came up with, I somehow knew Jo wouldn't let me get away with it. I imagined her banging on Aiden's door, forcing me into a dress, and dragging me out of the apartment while Aiden pulled my other arm to keep me there. Or, worse, she might show up at my house and tip off my parents.

No. She wouldn't really do that. But even the possibility that she almost might was enough to scare me into continuing along the path I'd already chosen. Besides, I *wanted* to go to the dance. I didn't want to tiptoe around Aiden's moods and bend to his will, to be the kind of girl whose boyfriend controls her every move. I wasn't that girl. I was smarter than that. I needed to remember to act like it.

After all the emotions and worries and extreme ups and downs of the past few days, I deserved a night to forget about everything and just dance.

I scooped a double cup of Cotton-Candy Crunch and a cone of Malted Magic with Loopy for Licorice on top, and smiled for the customers. "Lexa can ring you up right over there when you're ready," I said. We'd been so busy throughout the shift, I'd barely spoken to Lexa all day, but there would be plenty of time for chatting soon enough, when I became the odd extra on her involuntarily double date. I wondered if she ever resented Jo the way Jo resented her. If she did, she was far too sweet, or too smart, to show it.

Mr. Sugarman emerged from the back room, hefting a giant bag of gumdrops. "Joanna, help me refill this canister while Lexa takes care of these fine folks, and then you both can skedaddle.

Wouldn't want you turning into pumpkins before the ball even starts." He winked so kindly, it made me almost sad.

We topped off the gumdrops, then I clocked out and texted Aiden **hey** and **how was your day**, but when I climbed the front steps to Jo and Eric's house twenty minutes later, he still hadn't responded. Okay. So he was angry. There was nothing I could do about it now. I resolved to let that be his problem and try not to let it ruin my night.

"Hiiiii!" Jo cried, throwing her arms in the air as I let myself in, and immediately I could tell she'd been bouncing-off-the-walls hyper for hours. Eric's eyebrows, when he turned to greet me, confirmed it. He stood at the stove, dishing out what appeared to be at least his second helping of spaghetti.

"You hungry, Bumble Bee?" Before I could nod, he was already taking down a clean bowl for me. He heaped it with pasta while I got myself a fork. Their mom's spicy tomato sauce smelled amazing as usual. Dr. Metmowlee spent a full weekend each September in an epic sauce-making marathon, cooking down hundreds of plum tomatoes in a kitchen thick with steam and Nina Simone. Inevitably we all would get put to work, chopping and stirring and prepping the endless mason jars. I realized with a pang that last year's canning days had probably been my last—that when it happened this year, it would happen without any of us. We'd be eating inferior sauce stuck to overcooked noodles in our new dining halls with our new friends, hundreds of miles apart. Or I'd be here, but with Aiden, only stopping by this house when Jo and Eric came home between semesters, if they came home at all. Maybe they would fill their breaks with internships and adventures, like Kyle was doing to avoid our house. I banished the thought from my brain.

"Nice apron," I said to Eric.

"You like it?" He looked down at the vibrant lip-print fabric with *KISS THE COOK* across the chest. "It's a gift from our gram."

"A gift for *me*," Jo clarified.

"But it seemed like more my style," Eric said. My mouth was too full to respond.

Jo's phone chimed with a text, and from the small, private smile she gave when she saw it, I could only assume it was from Sydney. My own phone stayed silent and still in my pocket, and I wondered what Aiden was doing right then, and what it would take to appease him.

Eric hoovered the last of his noodles. "I told Lexa we'd swing by in like an hour so her mom can take pictures."

Jo's thumbs paused above her screen. "Gosh, does that leave her enough time to get pretty?"

Eric ignored the snark and dumped his dishes into the sink. "Lexa always looks pretty," he said. Even Jo couldn't argue with that.

I took a shower to rinse off the workday grime, wrapped myself in one of Jo's thick towels, and returned to her room. She was wearing a soft peach dress I'd never seen before, and I wondered what day she'd gone shopping. I felt a pinch of sadness that she hadn't invited me to go with her, and that if she had,

I'd most likely have said no. I was glad I was here for tonight, at least. However cranky Aiden might get about it, this had been the right way to go.

She twirled, showing it off. "You look gorgeous," I said. "That dress is perfect."

"Thanks. There's yours." She nodded toward the bed, where the long blue dress I would borrow was laid out next to a curled-up Stella, who narrowed her eyes as I approached. The last inch of her tail flicked once with disdain.

I picked up the dress by its hanger and froze as Jo's hand touched my arm. She ran her fingers over the bruises Aiden had left on my bicep, and I held still, barely breathing, as I waited for her to react. The marks had faded a lot over the past two days, but I should have known Jo would still notice them. Of course I'd known. Maybe I had even wanted her to.

Her hand dropped. "I can cover these up pretty well with concealer, I think. My skin is darker than yours but that shouldn't matter too much for arms, especially with the lights off. I don't even see the ones on your neck anymore."

I exhaled. She thought they were hickeys. I was relieved and disappointed. Relieved I didn't have to lie any further, disappointed my best friend could no longer see my whole truth.

I put on the dress, clipped my hair back in a twist, and watched while Jo camouflaged the bruises. I let her talk me into mascara and lip gloss—"Just a touch," she said, "look up"—and soon we were ready to go. I examined myself in the mirror. I looked good. Even though I was three inches taller than Jo and flatter, the dress fit me perfectly. I wished Aiden could see me in it. I snapped a photo and hit send. **Makeup by Jo**, I wrote, and tucked the phone into my purse.

We went downstairs, where Eric was waiting, wearing a pale pink shirt under his dark gray blazer. His hair was still wet from the shower, with comb marks running through it, and when Jo pushed us together for a picture, I was hit by the soap-and-cedar scent of his skin. Jo leaned in beside me and we all pressed close for a selfie. "Too freaking cute," she declared. She bent to strap on her shoes.

Jo held out her hand and Eric forfeited the car key. "You want shotgun?" he asked as we followed her to the Wildebeest.

"Nah, I'll take the back. Less chance of someone seeing me riding with a newly licensed driver."

"Ah, right: the Rules." He held open the car door for me and waited while I slid inside. "You look really nice," he said, and I looked up in surprise.

Jo started the engine. "Damn right she does!" She winked at me in the rearview as she adjusted the mirrors and Eric buckled himself into the front seat. I blushed with happiness. My friends were the best.

At Lexa's house, we got out of the car and dutifully posed for hundreds of pictures while Lexa's mom swooned over all of us and Lexa apologized profusely. I could see why Lexa was embarrassed, but in truth none of us minded—in fact, it was kind of fun. Every game of dress-up should have an appreciative audience.

Jo and I stood to the side as the photo shoot ended with a few dozen couple shots. We watched as Lexa's mom shouted instructions for the position of Eric's arm around Lexa's waist and the tilt of Lexa's chin. "Are you nervous?" I asked Jo.

"I'm ready," she said.

"Now kiss!" Lexa's mom cried, and I looked away as they leaned in to comply. Jo smiled right at them, but her attention seemed elsewhere. "Ooooh," Lexa's mom said. "That one's going on Facebook."

When we got to Sydney's, Jo jumped out to get her and Eric climbed between the front seats to squeeze into the back between Lexa and me. I leaned forward to watch as Jo rang the doorbell and Sydney stepped outside, holding something white that she presented to Jo. Jo laughed and held out her arm, and Sydney tied the thing to Jo's wrist. They got in the car and Jo showed off what it was: a bouquet of paper unicorns, hand-drawn with black ink and fastened into a corsage. I was impressed.

"I wasn't sure what kind of flowers would match her dress, but unicorns go with everything," Sydney said. She looked arty and sophisticated in a simple black dress that offset her still-winter-white skin and the blondness of her short, asymmetrical hair. Jo beamed at her in a way that made my heart ping with gladness, and I wished Aiden were here to look at me that way too.

I took out my phone as Jo cranked up the music and pulled away from the curb, and saw he had finally texted back. **Wipe it off**, the message said. **You look slutty**

My vision blurred. I closed my eyes, bit my lip, and felt the world swirl around me until Eric's hand on my arm brought me back to where I was. "You okay?" he asked softly.

I nodded, and found I meant it.

I powered off the phone and let out my breath. Fuck it. Fuck Aiden. Fuck his need to control me and his jealousy and his fits. I looked good. I felt great. I was out with my friends, we were seniors, it was spring, and I was about to hit the dance floor like nobody's business. Especially not his.

THIRTY-FOUR

FREEDOM AND GIDDINESS BLOOMED IN MY CHEST AND filled up my brain like helium. By the time we walked into the darkened gymnasium, passing under balloon archways and through the streamer-laden foyer, I was high on the elation of letting it all go. I was sick of twisting and contorting every awful thing Aiden did into the shape of something borderline acceptable. That text had been horrible, and I didn't have to put up with it tonight.

The room pulsed with each beat of the vibrating bassline that pulled us out onto the dance floor. My friends jerked, bounced, and grooved with abandon all around me, and I twirled and dipped and floated free from every shitty thing that had ever happened. We were sweaty and smiling and beautiful and here. There was nothing but this moment, this everything.

My heart surged with deep love for each familiar face that surrounded me—Jo, Eric, Lexa, and Sydney, but also Krystal and Eleanor, that girl from my junior-year psych class, even Tyson and Cicily and Sharla/Shyla/Shwhatever. And the less familiar faces, too. These people who had been my comrades or nemeses or background extras for the past four years, who would soon go off in their own directions, be part of their own new worlds. I wanted to pull them all close to me and hold on tight. How could I not have treasured every second I'd spent near each one of them? How could I not have realized how limited and precious our time together was, until we had only a few short weeks of it left? These near strangers, these sort-of friends, they'd slogged through years of torture alongside me, and now, in a flash, they would be gone.

But we still had tonight. Tonight would be endless.

We danced, danced, danced, and I beamed at Jo and she shouted something I couldn't quite make out over the music, but it didn't really matter because her huge, happy grin said it all. A slow song came on and I watched as she and Sydney moved together, Sydney sliding her arms up around Jo's neck, Jo circling hers around Sydney's waist, as if they had always belonged there. Sydney tipped her head toward Jo's and said something into her ear that made Jo's cheeks flush with pleasure, and they were so obviously into each other, so clearly perfect together, I couldn't even be jealous. I had never been so glad to be wrong.

I turned to walk off to the sidelines and there was Eric, heading straight toward me. "May I have this dance?" he asked.

I took his arm. "But of course." We positioned ourselves near but not-too-near Sydney and Jo. "Where's Lexa?"

"With Zehra and Marie. I think there's some junior-class drama going down."

"Ah." I looked around at the couples rocking back and forth to the music, some glued close together, others seemingly ready to spring far apart the second the song would release them.

"I know Jo kinda dragged you into this, but I'm really glad you're here," Eric said.

"Me too," I admitted, shifting my gaze back to his face. His hand pressed harder against the small of my back, and for one confusing second I thought he was guiding me in for a kiss, but instead he held on and tilted me back in a dip, and pulled us both upright, laughing.

"It's like a trust fall," I said, when I'd recovered from the head rush. He dipped me again, farther down this time, then sent me spinning at arm's length and curled me back in toward him. We spun and dipped and goofed our way across the gym, twirling faster and sillier from one song to the next, until my face hurt from smiling so hard.

"Air," I gasped when we reached the side doors, and Eric led me outside, where a cool blast of freshness welcomed us into the night. The relative quiet and moonlit calm were so jarringly different from the chaos inside, it took my brain a few seconds to adjust. It felt like we had stepped into another dimension.

This was not the same old courtyard from my school-day experiences, smelling of hot lunch and gym clothes, spotted with sophomores lounging between classes. Although I could make out the silhouettes of a few other people here and there, and see the glow of someone's cigarette less than twenty feet away, it seemed like our own private world.

I slipped off my shoes to give my soles some relief, and balanced on one foot while I wiggled my uncaged toes. With my feet bare and Eric's clad in his signature Sauconys, we were almost the same height, although in reality I was half an inch taller, at least. I wobbled to one side, knocking my shoulder against his, and giggled as he mimicked my one-legged pose and bumped right back into me.

This was why I loved him: Eric was *fun*. He was fun and mischievous and smart and goofy, and one of the most kind-hearted people I knew. I always felt safe, and safe being myself, when I was with him. He was so beautiful and so good. I couldn't believe how much I was going to miss him next year.

He reached out both arms to steady me. "Bee," he said.

"Eric," I said, imitating the sudden seriousness of his tone, but before his name was fully out of my mouth, I knew—knew I had always been right to love him, knew he could feel this thing between us too.

My heart pounded faster and blood rushed to my brain, and before I could stop to think, I leaned forward, lips parted, to kiss him.

He stiffened and I hesitated right at the moment our lips touched, the softest brush of skin on skin, no more than the opening words of a question I had for so long wanted to ask. Before I could lean in fully or pull away, Jo's voice cut through the roaring in my ears. "I'll check outside!" Eric's hands dropped from my arms and the door banged shut and there was Jo, standing beside us. "There you are! What are you guys doing out here, making out?"

My chest seized but she laughed and I realized she was kidding. "Lexa's been looking all over for you," she told Eric. I stared down at my feet to avoid both their faces, squinting to sharpen the image of my toes in the darkness. My skin felt awash with fresh shame. What had I just done?

The doors swung back open and out tumbled Lexa, with Sydney close behind. Lexa sidled up next to Eric and tucked herself under his arm. She nestled against him, tiny even in her high heels, and looking exactly like she belonged there. Relief crept into Eric's expression and my stomach filled quickly with rocks. What had I been thinking, forcing myself on him like that? I was supposed to be his friend.

"Let's do the photo booth!" Lexa said, including me in her smile, oblivious to my horrendous betrayal. Jo agreed for all of us while flashing me an eye-roll, and it was so normal and unsuspicious that I wondered at the simultaneous malfunctioning of her twin radar and her best friend radar, that she couldn't sense my meltdown right beside her, or its cause. But then she grabbed Sydney's hand and of course I understood. She was engulfed in the shine of falling in love, could see nothing outside that bright bubble that contained them. I had felt the same way with Aiden.

Oh shit. Aiden.

I followed after Lexa and Eric in a daze, but Jo's arm shot out to stop me. My whole body tensed, waiting for her admonishment.

"Whoa there, Cinderella," she said, and pointed to the ground. "Don't forget your shoes."

THIRTY-FIVE

I BEGGED OUT OF SQUEEZING INTO THE PHOTO BOOTH with them and excused myself by ducking into the ladies' room instead. I hid in a stall, examining the initials and affirmations scratched into the beige paint, trying to distract myself from facing what a shitty friend, shitty girlfriend, and shitty person I had become. It didn't work.

If Jo hadn't stepped outside at that exact moment, I would have kissed Eric for real. As it was, I'd already technically kissed him for sort of, and that sort-of kiss contained so much pent-up hope, such desperate longing for a version of my life so impossibly different from the one I had, it was dangerous to let myself think about what had almost been. Besides, that line of thinking was delusional. What had almost been was *nothing*. Nothing but an even larger disaster than the one I'd already caused.

Thank god Jo had interrupted us before I could fully go through with it—or before Eric was forced to embarrass me further by pulling away to stop it. I couldn't believe I had dragged him into that. I felt like total scum.

But I couldn't hide out in the bathroom forever. The dance would be over in another hour, and spending the rest of it locked in here would only draw Jo's attention to my absence. I released myself from the stall, washed my hands slowly, thoroughly, and leveled with my reflection above the sink. What Lexa and Aiden didn't know wouldn't hurt them, but I at least owed Eric an apology for throwing myself at him. The traitor in the mirror agreed.

I found him in the lobby, near the refreshments table, standing mercifully alone. He was staring at a tray of cookies that had been decorated with way too much school spirit. If my stomach weren't already aching from the thought of what I'd done, that muddy teal and gold-ish frosting would have sent it churning.

"Hey," I said.

It was subtle, but I saw him flinch. "Hey," he said back.

I had never felt awkward around Eric in my life, but I was making up for it tonight in spades.

He shifted his weight from one foot to the other. "Bee, I—"

"No," I cut him off. "I'm sorry. I am so, so sorry and I feel like such a jerkwad—I don't even know what I was thinking. I'll understand if you need to avoid me forever, but can we please just pretend it never happened? I swear it will never happen again."

Eric stared at me for an endless moment, then pressed his lips together and nodded. "Okay." He looked like he wanted to say something more, but didn't. I stood there, miserable in the knowledge I might have ruined everything good between us. A bouncy, happy pop song blared behind me. It felt like an attack.

Lexa appeared and slid her arms through both of ours. "Hey, you guys. Oooh, cookies!" She released my elbow and helped herself to one of the nauseating treats. "They're our school colors! Too cute. I bet that was Cicily's idea." If she noticed that neither Eric nor I seemed capable of responding, she didn't comment. She wiped the crumbs from the corner of her mouth and looked up at him. "Dance with me?" Eric nodded and Lexa reached for my hand. "Come with us."

I forced my voice to sound normal. "I'm taking a breather. I'll join you guys in a bit."

Lexa gave my hand a squeeze. "I know you miss Aiden. It sucks he couldn't come."

Tears pricked my eyes. "Thanks," I managed, and watched them walk away. She was right. I did miss Aiden, desperately. Standing alone in that stupid lobby, overwhelmed by guilt and regret, I wished so hard that I could fold myself against him, feel the warmth of his body and the sturdiness of his touch, as he wrapped his arms around me and made everything all right. If we had only been together, the way we were meant to be, none of the rest of tonight would have happened.

Not being near him felt suddenly unbearable. I had to get out of there and find my way to his side.

I turned away from the snack table and, as if by magic, there he was. Like I'd conjured him by wanting it so badly.

I blinked to clear the illusion but no, he was real, this was real, my own twisted fairy tale, complete with a prince strolling in under a wobbly balloon arch. I ran toward him. "Aiden!"

He gave a one-shouldered shrug. "Surprise."

I pulled him into the dark of the gym before any chaperones could spot him. In his T-shirt, jeans, and leather jacket, he didn't exactly fit in with the semiformal crowd. "I'm so happy to see you," I said over the music. "I was just—" He silenced me with a kiss. His tongue thrust into my mouth and rammed against mine and I leaned back to get some space, my body realizing before my brain did that something was off. He swayed like we were sailing on a boat across the ocean. I put my hands against his chest to steady us both. "Have you been drinking?" I asked.

"Maybe." He flashed a smile that was almost a sneer. "None of your business."

But I could taste it now, and see it. He was drunk.

This was bad. I had to get him out of here before he caused a scene and got noticed. I kept my hands on his torso and guided him toward the door.

"What about you, what have you been doing? Having fun with your little friends on the dance floor? You like shaking your ass for the high school boys? Rubbing it against them and proving you're a slut?"

He swung his hips back and forth in an awful imitation, and I looked away, furious, but that spark of fury was doused with guilt before it could turn into a flame. It sputtered into nothingness with barely a hiss of protest as I pushed open the door and stepped into the courtyard.

I'd deserved that. I deserved his anger and his jealousy and his horrible accusations. Everything he was saying about me was, in some way, true. He was drunk, but he was right.

I moved away from the doors, into the darkness. He followed. "Outside! Good idea. First you hide me from your family, now you're hiding me here, too. Do I embarrass you? Are you embarrassed to be seen with me? You're too good for me now, is that it?"

I put my hand on his arm, trying to calm him down and stop the shouting, but he shook me off. "Aiden, don't—"

The slap was such a shock, I almost didn't feel it at first. The ache in my jaw and the sting on my cheek were more surprising than painful. Mostly what I registered was the hot burn of shame.

He reached back and hit me again with a *crack*. This time, I felt it, every bit of it, and with a rush of terror, I felt how far he was from done. I had to make it stop. "Aiden, I'm sorry, I'm sorry, I'm so sorry," I said, but who knew if he could hear me over the shouting, because somehow now here was Jo, shoving in between us, pushing Aiden away from me, screaming at him, then at me, as I tried to pull her off him.

He was gone, he was gone, and she wouldn't let me go after him.

"Tell me this is the first time he's hit you," she growled, her grip pinning my arms like a straitjacket. But I couldn't do that, I was too sick of lying. I said nothing. "Fuck." The straitjacket released into a hug.

"It's not his fault," I said into her hair, numb from how inadequate the words were. "I know what it must have looked like, but it isn't like that. I shouldn't have—"

"*No.*" The fire in Jo's eyes could have burned the whole place down. "Listen to me. This is Not. Your. Fault. Do you hear me?"

I looked away. She didn't know Aiden. She didn't know *us*. She didn't know the half of what I'd done.

She pressed my cheek gently. "Does it hurt?"

I shrugged. Everything hurt. My stomach, my heart, my face, my pride. I was splitting open and bleeding love. Who knew if he would ever forgive me.

"You need ice," she said. "Stay right here. Do *not* move from this spot. Let me get the keys and we're leaving."

I gave in. I stood right where she'd left me, in the spot where I had stood with Eric, then with Aiden—the same spot where I'd ruined everything—and waited for whatever would happen next. I allowed the numbness creeping over me to sink inside, deep enough so I barely felt the relief of letting Jo take charge.

I waited where she'd left me and when she returned, I held the can of cold juice to my jaw as instructed and followed her back through the gym, where the music was still blaring and the dancers were still dancing and everyone else's life was continuing on as usual, uninterrupted by the fact of mine falling apart. I didn't feel grateful for the gift of invisibility. I didn't wonder what Jo had told Eric and Sydney, or how they would get home. I let her guide me out to the Wildebeest, lead me upstairs to her room, coax me into the ducky pajamas, and tuck me into her bed. I let the numbness swallow me whole in an approximation of sleep or death or whatever, because I knew—I'd lost Aiden and there was nothing left now but surrender.

THIRTY-SIX

JO'S HAND ON MY SHOULDER PULLED ME OUT OF A thick sleep with no dreams, no emotions, no sense of self. I didn't try to fight it—at first touch, I was awake and resigned to the reality of existence. But I held still for an extra moment, imagining her hand as an emotional paperweight keeping all my scraps and pieces from flying away. When she lifted it, I opened my eyes and, to my surprise, did not disintegrate.

"Hi," she said.

"Hi," I echoed. She quirked her lips but it wasn't a smile. "What time is it?" I asked.

"Ten thirty."

"Shit."

I scrambled to disentangle myself from the blankets but she was already shaking her head. "You're not going to work. I called Mr. Sugarman and asked Lexa to cover for you. You have a horrible stomach bug."

I sank back down. "Thank you." I knew she hated lying to

anyone about anything. I added it to my tally of debts.

It was hard to know where to even start apologizing. "I ruined your date with Sydney."

Jo gave me a pointed look. "Sydney should understand why I put my best friend first. And if she doesn't, then forget her."

That stung but I didn't have it in me to stand up to the attack. I looked away and saw my phone in her hand. "Aiden . . ." It was half question, half prayer. I couldn't finish either.

"He sent thirty-two texts," Jo answered, and I thanked whatever gods had carried him home safely when he had been in no state to drive. "I deleted them all. He's sorry and he loves you and you're a whore, how could you do this, he doesn't mean it, please forgive him, he loves you, where the hell are you, and it will never happen again. I told him damn straight it won't because if he doesn't stop texting or if I catch one whiff of him anywhere near you, I'm calling the police. I should be calling them anyway. This goes against every good instinct I have."

I shook my head so hard it almost came loose.

"I know," she said. "But if you talk to him, I will do it. And I'll tell your parents, too, though I really think we should tell them anyway. I'm serious about this. It's over. He can't come near you again."

Anger flickered inside me. Who gave her the right to decide about my life? But when I opened my mouth to argue, it came out more like pleading. "It's not like that. He was drunk and I upset him and I know it looked awful but you have no idea what he's been through. You've never given him a chance."

"Bee, *he hit you*. There's no world in which that is anything other than his fault. I have seen you at your shittiest, and even the very worst version of you deserves nothing but love."

"I kissed Eric," I said, and felt the truth hang heavy in the air around us. It was immediately too late to swallow it back down.

Jo hid her shock well but I still saw it skitter through her. "So what?"

There were both a million and zero answers to that. I didn't know how to give one.

"No, really: so what. So that means you deserve to get smashed in the face? Seriously, try to see this from my perspective for a second. What if it were me? What if you saw someone I love smack me across the face and shake me like he wanted to kill me? Come on, picture it right now, and tell me what you would do."

My brain conjured the image almost involuntarily—Jo, some guy, loud words, a punch—but as much as it hurt to even imagine it, this cartoon scenario was easy to shrug off. If that happened to Jo I would be furious and protective and want to rip the guy's balls off. But it wouldn't happen to Jo. Jo was different. Jo was not me. No one would ever treat her like that.

Jo would hate my thinking this—or maybe, probably, she knew it too—but I wasn't her costar, I was the best supporting actress. It may have seemed like we were skipping arm-in-arm through life, but I had always skipped double-time just to keep up. Life came easier for Jo. She was charismatic and interesting and good at whatever she tried, including things where she wasn't really trying—like when we'd both played clarinet in the elementary school band and I practiced and practiced because I loved clarinet, and Jo, who'd wanted trombone, barely touched it and became first chair.

It wasn't like that for me. All my life I'd worked to get good grades, follow the rules, keep things neat, make people happy. I did some extracurricular this and some AP/honors that, worked my job at the Shack, and kept pace with Jo, but I didn't excel at any of it—I labored over it, hard, and got the job done. The first thing in my life that had come truly easily was being with Aiden.

And now I was failing at that, too.

I twisted his ring on my finger and avoided meeting Jo's gaze. "He didn't want to kill me," I mumbled. She was always so hyperbolic. The strikes hadn't even left bruises.

"Bee. Please listen." As if I had another choice. "You want to find a way to blame yourself because that would make this a thing you can change and control, but I'm sorry, you can't control it. You can't control *him*. It's not what you did or didn't do, or the choices you made. It's the choice he made, and that choice is unacceptable."

I wondered what it would take to get her to stop talking. If I waited long enough, she would have to.

"Even if you fucked Eric on the dance floor in front of Aiden and all of us, that wouldn't make it okay for him to hit you. You know that. I know you know that. How can I make you believe it?"

I didn't answer. It was just like Jo to assume she could swoop in and decide things with a few magic words that would pull me back into step alongside her, wagging my tail, like she knew best—like she was some kind of authority on Aiden and me and the nuances of our whole relationship. Like she knew better how to live my life than I did. Which, maybe she did. But it still wasn't up to her.

"You can't fix him, but you can walk away," she said.

I felt the hairs on my neck rise up like Stella's fur when she was extra pissed. "I don't want to walk away. And *you* don't get to control *me*, either."

"I know you don't want to." Her voice was so sad. "But I think you know in your gut that this isn't what you want either. He isn't who you want him to be."

I shook my head. It was pointless to try to make her understand.

Maybe everything with Aiden had been a huge, horrible mistake, but he was my mistake to make. Reason couldn't change that I loved him.

THIRTY-SEVEN

JO KEPT ME PRISONER FOR MOST OF THE DAY, HALF
taking care of me, half forcing me through an Aiden detox. She
ran me a bubble bath, cued up comfort movies and cute animals
galore, baked us raisin-free cinnamon rolls, and proffered other
food and beverages every time I so much as blinked. I couldn't eat
a thing. Just the smell of Dr. Ruben's coffee made me sick with
too many memories.

We didn't talk about Eric or the kiss, and I didn't see or hear
him around the house. As Jo wore me down with her anti-Aiden
pep talks—her research into teen crisis hotlines and classic abuser
behaviors; her wondering out loud if I might like to talk to her
mom about it too; her reasonable, rational arguments to which it
became easiest for me to just give in and nod along because she
clearly wasn't otherwise going to get off my back—I was grateful
to not have to deal with avoiding Eric, too. I took his absence as a
sign he felt the same way.

By late afternoon, Jo reluctantly agreed to let me go home to walk Rufus, on the conditions that I leave my phone's location tracker on so she could monitor that I went straight to my house and stayed there, and that I absolutely, under no circumstances, was allowed to make contact with Aiden. The third condition, that she would be coming over later so we could tell my parents about him together, effectively putting the nails in the coffin of the relationship and hammering it shut forever, I needed some time alone to figure out how to talk her out of.

I drove home with no music, under a sky thick with clouds, and let myself in the front door. Rufus was right there waiting for me, whining and panting with the kind of fear that could only mean a thunderstorm was approaching. I knelt so my face was even with his and sank my fingers into his fur to comfort us both. He leaned against me and licked my arm with so much gratefulness, need, and love, it collapsed the dam that had been holding back everything inside me. I cried real sobs, right there on the floor with my dog—cried for everything I'd ruined, everything I'd been wrong about, all I couldn't control. I cried until I was emptied and raw, then I clipped on Rooey's leash, let him empty out too, and led him back inside as the first fat raindrops fell. He trembled at a crack of thunder and I coaxed him upstairs where he wasn't allowed, so he wouldn't have to be alone while I curled up on my bed and counted my regrets.

If only this storm had come last night instead, so Eric and I couldn't have stepped outside. If only I hadn't sent Aiden that selfie, fishing for compliments, rubbing it in his face. If only I'd told my parents the truth about us and demanded they give him a chance. If only I'd stood up for our right to be in love. If only, if only, if only.

I calmed Rufus with one hand and checked my phone with the other, responding **Fine** to Jo's **Everything okay there?** and **A little better. Thank you so much for taking my shift** to Lexa's **You poor thing, how are you feeling????** I ignored her immediate **Don't even mention it. xoxox.** I had enough guilt about Lexa already.

How had things gotten to this place? Aiden had made me feel so bold and brave when we first met. Now I was literally curled up in a ball, the smallest, weakest, most pathetic version of myself. This wasn't the way things were supposed to be. We had started with so much passion, so much promise, but what had happened last night was truly messed up. I knew that. I knew it wasn't okay. But I also knew it could be different. I wanted to hit rewind, to go back and do our relationship over again. This time I would do it right.

I knew life wouldn't give me that chance, but maybe Aiden would. Maybe after some time apart, while Jo calmed down and Aiden and I both took a step back, cooled off, and had a chance to miss each other and remember everything that had been so good, we could hit the reset button and move forward, even better together than we were before. Neither of us wanted things to be like they were now, so maybe they didn't have to be.

I only had to convince Jo to not tell my parents yet. To give it some time, let things settle down, allow Aiden a chance to prove he wasn't the monster she had made him out to be. Yes, some monstrous emotions had emerged from him last night, and yes, he had to stop those from controlling him. But he could do that. *We* could do that. He would confront his anger before it built up too far. I would never again push him to the brink.

If Aiden even wanted that chance. Jo's threats had been effective—he hadn't tried to reach out again. Maybe he was scared she really would call the cops, although surely they couldn't press charges if I refused to testify. But the fear I had messed up so badly that he was done with me, done with us, and this was all the excuse he needed to walk away forever, had been churning inside me all day. It settled in my gut like layers of silt, heavy and horrible and part of me now.

Maybe this was for the best. Maybe I was delusional and we were damaged beyond repair. I should let him disappear, hand my life and my broken heart over to Jo, let her and my parents take over my fate. What did it matter what happened to me next if Aiden didn't want me back anyway?

Rufus whimpered and I leaned over the side of the bed to tuck my arm around him and cuddle him close. And then I realized. Aiden wouldn't do this. He would never let me go. That couldn't be the truth of what was happening. I turned back to my phone and scrolled through the settings. Jo had blocked his number.

I hit unblock and immediately it buzzed with a message from Jo, as if she were watching me. **On my way over.** It was 5:53. My parents would be here soon too. If I was lucky, Jo would arrive first.

Rufus and I were halfway down the stairs when the doorbell rang. He barked and ran ahead of me, tail wagging. I opened the door to let her in, and there he was.

"Aiden." My voice caught in my throat as I stepped into his arms, my heart beating his name. When I pulled back, my face was wet with rain and tears. His cheeks didn't look any drier. I wanted to kiss away everything that had happened between us, but we were already running out of time. "You can't be here," I told him. "You have to go."

"No." He grasped both my hands in his. "We need to talk. I know you're upset, but please don't push me away. I'm sorry. I was drunk, I was mad, and I was wrong. You have to give me another chance. I swear I'll do whatever it takes to prove I'll never hurt you again."

I shook my head. That wasn't it. "Jo will be here any minute now, and my parents, too."

Aiden stood straighter. "Good. I want to prove it to them, too. We're done hiding and sneaking around. Let me talk to them. Let them see who I really am. They can't stop us from being in love."

Maybe not, but Jo would try. "Aiden, listen. Jo will call the cops and tell my parents, and they'll never let me see you again. You have to stay away until I convince her. If she sees you, it's over. You have to go, now."

I tried to take a step backward to demonstrate my point, but he held on tight. Despite everything I knew to be true, his grip sent a quick dart of fear through my heart. "I'm not leaving. I won't leave you." I could see in his eyes that he meant it. "Fuck Jo. Fuck the cops. We belong together. I need you. Please don't do this to us. I love you. Just talk to me, please."

The wet streets amplified the sound of every car that approached, and with each one, my panic mounted. In a matter of seconds, the next car would be Jo's. But it was clear that the more I begged, the more stubborn he would become. My brain spun with desperation. I had to make him leave.

He moved his hands around my waist. "Don't tell me we're through."

I said the one thing I could think of that would force him to walk away. It was the only way to protect him. The only way to save us. I could beg his forgiveness later. First I had to get him out of here, now. "I kissed someone else."

Confusion and anger flashed across his face, mixed with disbelief. I steeled myself, waiting for him to lash out, even hit me, but he stood stock-still and soon his eyes contained only sadness. "Why?"

I shook my head, not trusting myself to answer. My eyes filled with too many tears to let go, blurring my vision almost completely as he turned and walked away. I wanted to run after him and kiss away our mistakes. To beg him to come back, take me with him, forget the past. But I couldn't do any of that. I couldn't even cry. I watched as Aiden pulled on his helmet, swung his leg over Ralph, and took off without looking back.

Too fast. My heart accelerated with him as he shot up the street, speeding into the raindrops and away from my life. He was gone in an instant but I could hear him, faster and faster, when he should have been slowing down to pause for the stop sign at the end of my street. I ran off the stoop and into the storm, my footsteps pounding over the screech of tires, the crash of metal, and somebody's shouts of "Watch out, watch out!"

Not until Jo wrapped her arms around me and pulled me back to earth did I realize the person screaming was me.

THIRTY-EIGHT

PERHAPS THE RULES OF TIME AND SPACE CONTINUED on for the rest of the world, but not for me. Not for Aiden. One minute Jo's arms were holding me back, holding me in, anchoring me down through the blur of sirens, shock, and flashing red lights in the rain. The next minute I was squinting against the cruel, harsh light of the hospital waiting room, wondering at the styrofoam cup of water in my hands, obeying when my mom said, "Sit here," watching as she spoke with the police officers, the receptionist, the nurses. I registered warmth to my left and the faint scent of rosemary-mint shampoo, and Jo must have followed us here in her car because there she was, leaning against me—or had she been here, holding me up, all along?

It wasn't real. Nothing was real. It couldn't be real.

If Jo spoke, I didn't hear it, I heard only the sounds of shoes. The squeak of a nurse's sneakers and the click of the receptionist's heels and the sigh of Aiden's father's footsteps as he emerged through the sliding doors with a doctor, shook her hand, nodded twice, then stood alone, looking as lost and stunned as I felt. My mother's steps sounded steady and firm as she crossed the linoleum and touched his arm, offered a cup of coffee she had procured out of nowhere, and listened to whatever he was saying, too far away and too unreal for me to hear it. I wondered who was looking after Alex and Kendra. Aiden wouldn't like it if his siblings had been left alone.

Mom crouched in front of me, her words performing loop-de-loops on their path from her lips to my ears.

Medically induced coma
Next few hours will be critical
Fractures
Swelling
Internal bleeding
Broken
Can't rule out paralysis
Traumatic brain injury
Risk of seizures
Possible long-term damage
Cognitive impairments
Severe
Lucky
Nothing to do but wait.
Only one word mattered: *alive.*

THIRTY-NINE

I MUST HAVE SLEPT BECAUSE I AWOKE TO THE SNAP OF the window shade rolling up and an awareness of my mother bustling around the room. She laid a hand on my shoulder. "Better hurry up or you're going to be late."

I squinted at her through swollen eyelids. "What?"

"For school," she clarified. "Dad will drop you off but you'd better get a move on."

I let my lids drop shut. "I'm not going to school."

"Yes, you are." She gave me a gentle shake. "Your staying in bed won't help anyone."

I rolled away from her touch but I didn't have the energy to fight her. What was the point? It didn't matter where I was or what I did. She was right: Whether I got up and went to school or stayed in bed forever, I couldn't fix what I had done to Aiden. Nothing could. I might as well do as I was told and zombie forward.

I stood up, made my bed, brushed my dry, scuzzy tongue, and wished I believed in a god so I could pray to it. Not that I even knew quite how. My mother had grown up Catholic but our family wasn't religious. I'd been to a Passover seder at Jo and Eric's aunt's house, but I remembered the zing of horseradish and the hunt for the afikoman better than I remembered the prayers. Cicily and her moms had taken me to church a few times after Saturday sleepovers way back when we were friends, but I'd paid more attention to the dust motes dancing in the rays of stained-glass sunlight than to the chorus of "Thy kingdom come, Thy will be done." Even if I knew the rest of the words to go with that refrain, it wasn't what I wanted anyway—I wanted *my* will to be done. I wanted everything that had happened last night and before to be *un*done. But no prayer to any god could make that happen.

A single word formed and echoed in my brain, containing every hope I dared not release into the universe. *Please.* It was better to loop on that helpless plea than to remember the last words I had said to him, the crumpled, broken look on his face, the way I'd crushed his heart and pushed him away, pushed him toward this fate, when all he had wanted was to fix us.

I couldn't think about that. I couldn't think about brain damage, paralysis, broken bones, death. I couldn't think about bruises, his or mine, on the surfaces of our skin or in our hearts. I couldn't think about fear, pain, hurt, guilt, sadness, anger, or love, couldn't allow myself to feel any of it. Because if I felt any of that, I risked also feeling the horrible, unwelcome, and unspeakable thing that had snaked beneath it the moment he'd turned away: relief.

That was the worst feeling of all.

***

It would be easier if he were dead.

I swallowed against the tightness in my throat as I pushed toward my locker, ignoring the whispers, ignoring the stares. I didn't care what they were saying. I didn't care what anyone thought. I only cared that Aiden—

No. I couldn't even think his name. I had to focus on putting one foot in front of the other, on moving forward and making it through this minute, this hour, this morning, this day, while knowing what I'd done.

My stomach lurched but there was nothing inside it to heave out. As soon as I'd stepped out of the car I had thrown away the breakfast Dad insisted I take with me. Eating was impossible. All of this was impossible. Aiden was on life support; I couldn't chew and swallow cinnamon-sugar toast.

I breathed in and tried to force the sounds of the accident out of my brain. *He's still alive*, I reminded myself. *He might wake up. He might forgive me.* It was too many maybes, all followed by unanswerable then-whats.

"Hey, Betts," someone said. I kept walking. "Bee," she called again. "That ring you wear—is it from Aiden?"

I stopped. Turned. Stared.

My fingers flew to the ring on my right hand, shielding it from Cicily's gaze. I couldn't believe she'd asked me that. I couldn't believe she had the nerve to even speak his name.

I would not give her the satisfaction of watching me disintegrate. "Mm-hmm," I managed. The ring stayed on my finger but

219

I felt it clenching my heart.

"You guys seem really cute together," Sharon/Shareen said. She tucked a lock of hair behind one ear. It hit me that she wasn't trying to be cruel.

Oh god. They don't know.

"Is he coming again after school today?" Cicily winked in case I missed her disgusting double entendre.

My mouth tasted like stomach acid. I tried not to think about vomit. "No."

The third girl's gold pendant gleamed against her brown skin. "Where did you even meet him? I need to find me a guy like that." She elbowed Cicily. *"Vroom, vroom."*

I shook their laughter out of my head. I couldn't have this conversation, couldn't pretend it was okay. Couldn't act like the ground was still solid beneath me.

I turned around and fled, running blindly through the hallway, bag bouncing, eyes burning, until I slammed into the one person who didn't have the sense to move out of my way.

"Bee . . ." Eric wrapped his arms around me, and the thin glass walls that had been holding my heart together since last night splintered and shattered to the floor. I collapsed into the warmth of his strong, sturdy hug and soaked up the sympathy I didn't deserve from the last person I should be allowing myself to embrace. "I didn't think you'd be coming to school. Jo said—I'm glad to see you. I'm sorry, this is horrible. I don't even know what to say."

I hid my face against his shoulder and we both said nothing, which was all that was left. He held on until I pulled back and saw the halls around us were almost emptied out. The bell must have rung, but somehow I'd missed it.

"Does Jo know you're here?" he asked.

I shook my head. "I haven't seen her. You should go. I'm making you late."

"Please. It's only homeroom." He took my bag and steered me toward my locker. For the millionth time in however many hours, it was easier to let someone else make the decisions. Eric didn't ask questions or try to hurry me along; he just stood by patiently while I opened my locker, stared at my belongings, and tried to remember what I was doing there. Being in school at a moment like this seemed ludicrous, but this was my life. I was stuck in it.

I took out the nearest notebook without caring which one it was, shut the locker, and followed Eric to my classroom. He paused with his hand on the doorknob. "You'll get through this," he said. "You're going to be okay."

I didn't know if by "this" he meant first period or the school day or Aiden being in the hospital, possibly paralyzed or already dead. I didn't know if he was saying it to convince himself or me. It didn't matter. I nodded.

He opened the door and I stepped through it.

FORTY

WHEN HOMEROOM ENDED A FEW MINUTES LATER, JO was outside the door, waiting for me. "I'm getting you out of here," she said, and handed me my bag. "Let's go."

It was a nice gesture, but useless. "I can't skip. They'll call my mom." So far both my parents had given wide berth to the obvious fact of how much I'd disobeyed them, but of course that conversation was coming. I didn't need to add any twigs to the bonfire. My future was already up in flames.

"We're not skipping," she said. "I'm signing us out."

She needed to play rescuer and I needed to be saved, so I followed her to the office and watched, amazed, as she chatted with the secretary, accepted a pen and clipboard, and signed the checkout sheet with a flourish. No one else would get away with a stunt like that, but of course she could. Jo was magic. It probably never occurred to her the world might say no.

It never occurred to her I might say no, either.

We buckled into the Wildebeest. "Where to?" she said.

"Will you take me to the hospital?" I knew the answer but I had to ask.

"No way." Her voice was firm but she looked at me gently. "Even if I brought you there, they wouldn't let you see him," she added.

I leaned back.

"Your choices are: my house, diner, coffee shop, or park."

"Your house," I said. We drove there in silence.

I loved her. I hated her. She was all I had.

Stella mewled at us and wove her way between Jo's legs, glaring at me as though she knew I was responsible for this change in her routine. It felt good to be openly blamed for something, even by a cat, even for just existing. I crouched and ran a hand along her surprisingly sharp spine. She arched her back into my palm, half purring, half hissing, to convey I was barely worthy to pet her. Jo shut the refrigerator door somewhat hard, and Stella started and dashed into the living room.

Jo handed me a root beer. "Drink," she ordered. I twisted off the cap, put the bottle to my lips, and forced myself to take a swig. The sweetness and spice hit my tongue with startling intensity, and I could almost feel my blood moving faster through my veins, encouraged by the presence of calories. I lowered myself onto a stool and put one hand on the counter, suddenly faint from how long it had been since I'd eaten. Saturday night? Yesterday morning? I couldn't remember. Those moments seemed light-years away.

I took another sip and closed my eyes as I swallowed. I hadn't had root beer in ages, not since I had switched to coffee. It tasted like before. It tasted like who I used to be. The aftertaste lingered like a memory.

I drank the whole thing in small, slow sips, not looking at Jo until I was done. "Thank you," I said. She nodded.

"I don't know what to do."

"Me neither," she admitted.

I scraped the edges of the label from the bottle with my thumbnail, then destroyed the list of states that collected a five-cent deposit. The silence was punctured by the chime of Jo's phone. She checked it, typed something back, and sank onto the stool beside me. "Eric. Checking to make sure you got out okay."

"He's too nice."

"He loves you. We're both extremely worried."

I flicked Michigan onto the counter. "If you had any sense you would both stay far away."

Jo lifted her eyebrows. "Not true."

"It is true. I'm toxic. Being near me is toxic. You should run and save yourselves." I was just talking, it was nonsense, light-headed blabber, but the more I said, the more strongly I believed it.

"You're not toxic," Jo said. She sounded exhausted by the topic already.

"I am. Look at what I did to Aiden. He's the best thing that ever happened to me, and I hurt him so badly he might never wake up."

Her glare razored through my self-pity. "No, look what Aiden did to *you*. Look what he did to himself. He is far from the best thing that's happened to you. Come on. You know better than this."

Anger bubbled through me. Aiden was in a coma, he might die or be paralyzed or in other ways never recover, and Jo was talking shit about him. "You're glad. You're glad this happened. You want him to die." I sounded petulant. I didn't care. I almost wanted her to scream at me.

Jo exhaled a long, heavy breath and spoke slowly. "If this is what it takes to get him away from you, then okay, sure, I'm glad. I'm glad he broke his own bones before he could break yours. I'm glad the injuries he caused this time are to himself instead of you. I don't wish him dead, but I wish him out of your life for good, and if it will stop you from going back to him and letting him beat you again, I will go to that hospital and pull the plug myself. He's not good to you, Betts. He's jealous and possessive and abusive. You have bruises. I watched him hit you."

I blocked it out. "He loves me."

Her eyes went fierce. "*I* love you. Of all the humans in the world with whom I do not share DNA, I love you the most. You are my favorite. And I hate seeing you let him define who you are."

"As opposed to letting you define me?" I shot back.

"No!" she said. "Or, you know what? Yes. Yes, as opposed to that. Our friendships define who we are. *This* friendship defines who I am. Being best friends with you brings out all the best and weirdest, most creative and interesting and worthwhile sides of me, and it challenges me to be better and makes it okay that I'm flawed, and I hope I do that for you, too. I am ten million times better and stronger because of it, because of us. So yes, this friendship defines me, and because of it, who and what I am is *more*. A good relationship should do that too, but all I see in this one is you being diminished. He treats you like his possession and that's not the same thing at all. You're too boxed in to thrive and grow and make mistakes and be all the brilliant things you are. He is trying to contain you, and I don't know why you can't see how much you deserve to fly free."

The words knocked at my heart but I wouldn't let them in. I couldn't let them in. I spoke as calmly as I could. "I don't want to fly free. I want this. I want to be his. This is who I am now. I'm sorry if you don't like it, but tough luck."

We both stayed quiet for several minutes, and it seemed possible we might never speak again. I had one more thing to say, though. "It's your fault too," I told her. "If you hadn't threatened him, threatened us, I wouldn't have sent him away."

I kept my focus on the shredded bits of label on the counter, but I could feel her not moving, barely breathing, beside me. She held still until I almost wondered if she was still there.

When she spoke, the sound startled me. "Remember that song about the bears in the bed?"

I looked at her.

"Where the little bear complains and pushes all the other bears out, one by one, until she has the whole lonely bed to herself?" I nodded but she sang anyway, *"Ten bears in the bed and the little one says, 'I'm crowded! Roll over!' So they all roll over and one falls out. Nine bears in the bed and the little one says—*"

I nodded harder to stop her. "Yes. I get it. I remember."

Her eyes narrowed to a glare. "Well, I'm done rolling over for you, Baby Bear. This is it. I won't budge. You are stuck with me, we are getting you out of this, and I am not fucking letting you push me away."

I looked down but still heard her breath catch in her throat, a sound that was repeated in my own as the full force of what she was saying sank in, despite how hard I'd been trying to keep it all out. "Don't cry," I said to the floor.

She laugh-sobbed, and I looked up to see her eyes streaming. "I'm crying," she said. "Most definitely crying."

I choked out a laugh and a sob of my own. "Me too."

She hugged me. "I'm sorry he hurt you. I'm sorry I didn't know."

I squeezed back and whispered, "I'm scared."

FORTY-ONE

"BETTS." CICILY ENGULFED ME IN A SIDE HUG, HER hair invading my mouth, her perfume assailing my nostrils, an attack on my decision to not skip school again today. I stiffened and she pulled back. "I'm so sorry about Aiden. I had no idea. It's so awful. Are you okay? If there's anything I can do, I am completely here for you, just say the word. I can't believe it. This is so unbearably tragic."

"Thanks." I turned toward my open locker, hoping she would leave, but of course she didn't take the hint. I didn't need her faux-concern about his well-being added to the confusion and chaos inside me. I wished I could be as clear-headed about him as Jo, but with logic pushing me one way and my emotions hauling me the other, I was ripping myself apart in a brutal game of tug-of-war that would all be for naught if Aiden didn't come out of his coma anyway. Until that happened, I had to hold out hope. I needed to give him something to wake up for.

"I want you to know, I'm telling everyone it's not true. The part about why he did it. Because it isn't, right? I mean, you and Aiden, everyone could see you were so in love."

I flinched at the past tense. Thirty-nine hours since the accident and already Cicily was counting him dead. "I don't know what you're talking about."

Her mouth formed a glossy O. "Oh no, you haven't heard. I mean, they're just nasty rumors. You know how people love to gossip. Oh god, I'm so sorry. They're saying Aiden tried to kill himself because you made out with Eric, and that's why Eric broke up with Lexa on Sunday night, too. I heard she's devastated. You know, she hasn't come to school since. I'm sure she doesn't believe that part if she's heard it, though. You and she are friends, right? Have you talked?"

Eric broke up with Lexa? No, nothing out of Cicily's mouth could be trusted, even if part of it was almost, sort of true. Somebody must have seen me with Eric at the dance—although of course, I realized, everyone saw us dancing, and the rumors could also have sprung up from that, or even from our hug in the school hallway yesterday morning. It didn't take truth to get the gossip machine going. I wondered how much of it Lexa believed, how badly she hated me, how mortified Eric was for that rumor to be making the rounds. No wonder it felt like everyone in my lit class had been staring at me.

I squared my shoulders and looked her straight in the face. "Cee, I'm going to need you to fuck off."

Her eyes widened and narrowed in almost comic proportions. "What happened to you?" she asked softly.

"What *happened* to me? My boyfriend is in a fucking coma. I watched him almost die, and now you're standing here accosting me with stupid rumors and pretending that you care about the truth and my heart. What the fuck do you mean, what happened to me?"

Cicily shook her head slowly, sadly. "No, I mean before this. Before him."

I stared at her.

"We used to be friends."

"Yeah. Well. We grew apart, I guess," I said.

She nodded, like this brought new understanding she could finally comprehend. "I guess we did. I mean it, though—if you need anything from me, I'm here for you. I'm sorry."

She turned and walked past OJ, who'd been shifting from foot to foot, waiting for a turn at her own locker like it was the bathroom. She beelined for her combination lock and avoided looking in my direction. I appreciated that small dose of normalcy, and almost admired her ability to radiate discontent. The world didn't allow much space for female rage.

I closed my eyes and wondered if Aiden was still breathing.

I made it through Latin and found Jo before lunchtime, intercepting her on her way to the cafeteria and guiding her out to a picnic bench in the courtyard. The sun was bright but it was too windy and cold to be outside. Jo didn't complain. "Were you going to tell me about Eric and Lexa?" I asked.

"Yes." She rubbed her arms with both hands but shook her head when I offered my sweatshirt. "It didn't seem all that pressing compared to everything else. And I didn't want to add to your worries. Which it shouldn't. I think this was a long time coming."

"Poor Lexa."

Jo shook her head. "It was mutual. He was going to break it off but she brought it up first. She's not getting what she needs from him, or something. He claims they're going to stay friends."

I felt some tension inside me relax. Being with Aiden had conditioned me to automatically take the blame for everything, but it rang true that maybe this one thing wasn't about me. I may have kissed Eric, but he hadn't exactly kissed me back. I just hoped Lexa knew that—or, better yet, didn't know anything about it. "Is he doing okay?"

"Yeah. He's sad but I think worrying about you has eclipsed it."

We sat with that in silence until she grinned suddenly and waved at the glass doors to the cafeteria. Sydney pushed one open. "Are you guys getting lunch?" The wind whipped her hair around her face.

"Yes!" Jo called back. "Save us a seat?"

Sydney retreated inside and Jo looked at me. "Is that all right?" she asked.

"Yeah," I said. It was. I looked back at her, my best friend since second grade, the same girl I had loved, admired, teased, trusted, squabbled with, followed, supported, and leaned on all this time—yet also, of course, not the same girl at all. I'd been so afraid of how things between us were going to change, I'd nearly overlooked or forgotten that of course we'd both been changing all along. Our friendship had room for this change, too. There were so many uncertainties in my head and my heart, but Jo was not one of them.

We stood and she smoothed down her skirt. "Anyway, you know my brother. He'll be on to the next girl before we can blink. Though I told him, in my professional opinion, it might do him some good to be single for a while. Like maybe at least until the end of the week."

I half smiled as was expected but my gut twisted with a sharp pang, and I envied Jo's sense of time. For me, each minute had been lasting for hours; an hour stretched to span years. The end of the week seemed a lifetime away, not knowing whether Aiden would be in it, or what I would do if he lived.

I couldn't let myself think of the future. I couldn't let myself think of our past. I was spinning in the now, now, now of endless questions my brain didn't want me to ask.

I owed it to him to keep hoping. What I owed to myself would come last.

FORTY-TWO

THE TAP AT MY DOOR WAS SO SOFT AND UNEXPECTED, I almost didn't process it as a knock. I lifted my face off the pillow. The doorknob turned.

"May I come in?" It was unusual for Mom to even ask, but she still didn't wait for an answer.

I sat up and looked at the clock. It wasn't time yet for setting the table. It wasn't time yet for her to be home. She sat on the edge of my bed and I pulled my knees to my chest so my legs wouldn't touch her. I guessed it was time for a Talk.

"Aiden's father called," she said. Every muscle in my body went on high alert. I couldn't tell from her expression whether it was good news or bad. I almost didn't want to know. "He's awake."

She was watching for my reaction but I didn't blink or feel or move, only waited to hear more. There were a million *but*s that could follow that.

"There's a long road ahead, months of healing and physical therapy and rehabilitation to come, but based on what they can see today, the doctors are optimistic. He's going to pull through this. He's going to be okay."

I swallowed. I wanted to jump up and cry out and scream and laugh and release all my tears, but I didn't dare move, just in case this wasn't real, just in case by reacting I might change it. *He's going to be okay. He's going to be okay. He's going to be okay.* I waited for the hopes and fears wrapped so tightly around my chest to loosen, unspool, untangle, rethread. They didn't.

"There's a clinic in Arizona that specializes in recovery for these types of injuries, where he can get good care and be close to his mother. They'll be moving him there as soon as he's able." I flinched, knowing how Aiden wanted nothing to do with his mom.

Arizona. I could hear Jo's voice in my head saying, *Good. Good riddance*, but despite that, despite everything, I ached at the idea that he would be taken so far away from me.

My mother shook her head slowly. "He's very lucky. And we're lucky too. Thank god you weren't on that death trap with him. I can't even begin to let myself think about what could have happened to you."

But if I had been with him, none of this would have happened. He would have driven carefully. Neither one of us would have gotten hurt.

No. Now that he was awake, now that I knew for sure he would live, I could allow myself to admit it: I still would have gotten hurt. He hadn't been careful with me. He'd hit me. He'd manipulated me. He'd accused me of things I hadn't done and refused to accept my assurances. He'd held out his love like a test that was designed for me to fail, and made me work to prove again and again the truths he would never believe.

But I couldn't help it; I still loved him. I wanted to believe that from now on, things could be different for us. As pathetic as it made me, I wanted the impossible to be true.

"I'm sorry," I said, because I didn't know what else to tell her.

She sighed. "I know you can't begin to comprehend how terrifying it is to let your child grow up and go out into this world. Your father and I have always tried to set boundaries to help keep you and your brother safe. We've tried to help you learn good judgment and make smart choices. We thought we were doing well. But everything about this, about you and that boy, makes me wonder. How can I ever trust you again?"

I met her eyes. "You can't, Mom. It's not a matter of trust. My decisions about my life, my body, my future, have nothing to do with you. My choices are on me now. You have to let me make my own mistakes. Who I love is not up to you." Whether Aiden and I stayed together or not, I needed her to know that.

"I will not stand by and watch you throw your life away for him."

I looked away. "You don't know him," I said, but I was tired of defending him. Tired of the loop of my own emotions and excuses; tired of being a giant walking cliché. I knew better, of course I did. What I knew and what I felt were two deeply different things. I was tired of trying to reconcile them.

"The Aiden I remember had a lot of rage and entitlement—not the best combination in a young man. Those certainly aren't traits I want near my daughter."

I picked at the bedspread. "You don't think people change?" I wondered if I thought he truly could.

"Sometimes. Slowly. And I hope he'll get that chance. But not with you in his path."

We sat quietly, at a standstill. I swiveled the ring Aiden had made me. It was turning my finger green.

"I'm sorry for all the ways I've failed you," she said. "I do my best and sometimes it's not enough. I don't know what I could have done differently this time, but believe me, I stay up nights wondering and counting the ways."

My gut twisted with shame. It had never occurred to me that my choices and lies would feel like her failures.

She tucked her arm around me and I realized I was shaking. "I wish I could protect you from everything that hurts."

I let her hold me. I tried to imagine going back to him. I imagined staying away. "I wish you could too."

FORTY-THREE

I LEFT SCHOOL EARLY AND WALKED THREE BLOCKS IN the rain to catch the metro bus to the hospital. I didn't dare try Jo's self-sign-out trick, but I hoped I wouldn't need it—my last class of the day had a sub and I'd asked Eleanor to say "here" at my name if he bothered to take attendance. She'd agreed without asking questions, and I was grateful. Perhaps she could see I didn't feel like talking about it. Perhaps she had her own shit going on and didn't fully care about mine. Or maybe, I realized as the bus doors wheezed open and I climbed the damp steps and paid my fare, she was just being a good friend.

After so many days of time moving at a slower-than-glacial pace, the bus ride passed alarmingly swiftly and I found myself entering the hospital lobby, squinting under the fluorescent lights, realizing I hadn't thought through how I would even convince them to let me see him. But I was signed in without resistance and pointed toward Aiden's room, up two floors and down a beige-on-beige corridor lined with the rooms of other people living out tragedies or miracles of their own. I didn't pause to witness them. I passed through Aiden's doorway and everything else in the world disappeared.

He lay on the bed, eyes closed, body still, except for the rise and fall of his chest each time he breathed. My own breath went shallow as I took in the bruises on his skin, the needle in his arm, the bandages and the medical tape and the cast that held his leg together. All these signs of what it had taken to keep the boy I loved alive.

I stepped closer. Aiden's eyes opened slowly and he looked at me in a way that felt like he'd been watching me stand there all along.

"What are you doing here?" he said. His voice was as cold as his words.

I hesitated. I had been asking myself the same question again and again on the way over—asking and avoiding it, both. Now that I was here by his side, I finally knew the answer. "I came to say good-bye."

I slid the ring off my finger and set it on the table beside his bed. It made a soft *clink* that I felt like the turn of a key in my heart.

Aiden's eyes filled with sorrow. "Bee, no. Don't do this. I love you so much. You at least owe me another chance."

"I love you too," I said, because it was true. But I could see another truth now, one that in all my imaginings of us starting over and my hopes for how things would improve, I had tried so hard to deny: It would get worse. He would grow angrier and more controlling. He would hit me again, harder. Our lives would intertwine and it would be more and more impossible for me get away. I had to end it now. This was my new beginning.

I gathered all the strength I had and said, "And I don't owe you a thing." The words were electric in the air, and I could feel it now, everything Jo had tried to tell me. The truths I'd denied, the anger I'd suppressed. Fear of losing him was giving way to the urgency of reclaiming myself. It expanded in my chest like courage. "I love you more than I loved myself, and I'm done with that. I'm done with us. I thought that love could be enough and I was wrong, so wrong. But I am not the problem. You are. And you will never come near me again. That's what I came here to tell you."

His smile snaked up slowly, as calm and certain as that first smile he gave me, the one that literally took my breath away. "You'll regret it," he said.

I smiled back and kept breathing. "I already do. I regret I didn't do this sooner." I turned on my heel and walked away.

A rush of adrenaline powered me outside into the spitting rain. I zipped up my jacket, turned my face toward the sky, and allowed the sting of the raindrops to prove this was real, I was here, I had done it. It was over. I wanted to whoop and leap and throw up and hug Jo, but instead I blinked into the clouds, exhaled, and moved forward. I sank into a seat on the half-empty bus, stared across at the fogged-up windows, and let the fear and sadness I had been carrying for so long roll out of me in fat, silent tears. I mourned what I'd lost, mourned what he'd taken, mourned what I knew now could never have been. By the time the bus reached my stop, I felt stronger, lighter. I exited out the back, leaving the weight of it all behind me. I'd done it. I was free.

FORTY-FOUR

I REACHED THE SHACK SIXTEEN MINUTES EARLY, TOO soon to clock in, but I went inside anyway, tied on my apron, and prepared to face Lexa, rehearsing an apology in my head. I would quit this job after today, I decided, and let her have this place. I would find a new job, a fresh start for summer, somewhere that wasn't tainted by memories of him.

But Lexa didn't show. "Schedule change," Janice explained with a shrug, and I didn't ask her any more about it. In the shifts I'd worked with Janice before, she was friendly with the customers, but not especially so with me. She had a teenage kid at home and seemed to resent having to work with one, too.

I thought about texting Lexa to make sure she was okay, but if she was avoiding me on purpose, the least I could do was respect that. There would be plenty of time for apologizing later, if later she was willing to hear it. I pushed her out of my mind and fell into the rhythm of the shift.

The rain seemed to keep most of the drop-ins at bay—people

came in knowing what they wanted to buy and were uninspired to linger. That kind of efficiency was calming, and as I cut and weighed blocks of peanut butter fudge, packed a pint of Creamy Dreamy Caramel ice cream, rang up bouquets of lollipops, and wiped the counter until it shined, knowing this would be my last shift here ever allowed me to almost-nostalgically enjoy it. In the past two months, everything in my life had metamorphosed or exploded except this place, which changed with the day and season yet always stayed the same.

In the rockiness and limbo of senior-year uncertainties, I'd clung to Aiden, needing a sense of permanence. Maybe it was okay for some things to change.

I added it to the list of Things to Tell Jo in person tonight: one more of today's million revelations.

"You mind if I take a smoke?" Janice asked, disappearing without waiting for an answer. I nodded into the empty space and felt glad to be alone. But before I could fully relax into it, the entrance bells jingled and Eric came inside. I set down my cleaning rag. I hadn't seen him since I'd walked straight into him Monday morning, and it would be fair to say I had basically been avoiding him the past two days. From his tentative look as he glanced around at everything in the shop except me, it seemed safe to guess he'd been avoiding me too. I felt bad. He probably hadn't realized I'd be working.

"Lexa's not here," I said. "She switched shifts."

Eric cleared his throat and ran a hand through his hair, exposing the spot above his temple where, instead of jet-black, a patch always grew in white. It was usually masked pretty well by his haircut, but I loved that secret little imperfection. I used to joke it was the only way to tell him and Jo apart. "I know. I came to see you. I was hoping you'd have a minute to talk," he said.

For some reason this made me panic and I thought about inventing some task I had to tend to, but it was pretty obvious I wasn't busy. "Sure."

His shoulders relaxed, like he'd been bracing himself for me to say no. I tried to lower my defenses too. "I wanted to check if you're okay," he said.

I soaked up the warmth in his kind, familiar eyes, so similar to Jo's yet with a glister all his own, and felt how lucky I was to have these friends who loved me. "Yeah," I said. "I am. I will be." For the first time in a long time, I knew it was really true. "How about you?"

"You heard about me and Lexa," he guessed.

"I did. I'm sorry."

He acknowledged that with a grimace. "Don't be. I mean, it sucks. Lexa's great and I adore her, but it was never going to be more than what it was, you know? And I realized I want that. I want something more."

I nodded. Of course he did, and I had no doubt he would find it. I tried not to feel jealous of whatever lucky person got to have that with him at some point down the line, tried not to still wish it could be me. I was lucky too. I'd gotten to grow up beside him, to count him as my friend all this time. I needed to let that be enough and stop allowing myself to wonder what a real kiss with him would be like.

"Bee, listen. What happened the other night at the dance, between us—I know you don't want to talk about it, and after this we never have to, but I wanted to say, I wish it could have been different. That the timing and the circumstances could have been better for us both. You know?"

I did know. I wished that too. But I hadn't realized he felt that way.

I guess he saw the question in my eyes. "It wasn't just you," he said. "I wanted to kiss you. I thought you should know that."

My skin tingled with a slow, new awareness. I barely trusted myself to move. "Thanks," I said carefully. "That—that's really nice to hear." This day, this week—the past two months—had been too much of a roller coaster for me to say or do anything else. I knew better than to catapult into anyone else's arms, even Eric's. Especially Eric's. What I needed now was not a new boyfriend. What I needed now was my friends. But I was grateful he'd said that.

He looked almost pained. "I still want to kiss you. And I know the timing is lousy, still, for both of us. But I wanted to say, if you still want to kiss me too—I'll wait."

The warmth on the surface of my skin seeped inside. It felt a lot like hope. "I might," I said. "Not today. But maybe. Eventually. Yes."

He exhaled. A smile tickled my lips.

In my head Jo was laughing at both of us. A nice laugh. The best laugh. One I'd join in when I told her all this. One Eric would appreciate too.

Janice came in through the back room, bringing a jolt of reality and the smell of nicotine along with her. At the same time, the front door opened and a customer blew inside, shaking an umbrella in one hand and holding a toddler's hand in the other. Eric straightened. "I better let you get back to work, but I'm glad you're all right. I'll see you soon, okay?"

"Okay," I repeated. "Soon." I tipped my visor to him and he smiled, releasing my heart like a helium balloon. If there was more to come in our future, we would get there. No rush. I still got to have this gladness, this now.

I moved over to the ice cream station, where the mom was reading off flavors to her kid. "See any you'd like to try?" I asked and reached for a neon taste spoon. I waited for their decision and my stomach dropped as the crackle and roar of a motorcycle approached. A chill crept up my neck and the muscles in my throat went tense. I forced myself to relax. The motorcycle passed.

It wasn't him.

I wouldn't be afraid.

That was over.

Truly over.

I was free now.

He was gone.

I dipped the spoon into the carton of Baby That's Bittersweet and offered the woman a taste.

RESOURCES

LOVE IS RESPECT

Chat at loveisrespect.org

Text **loveis** to 22522

Call 1-866-331-9474

NATIONAL DOMESTIC VIOLENCE HOTLINE

Chat at thehotline.org

Call 1-800-799-SAFE (7233)

ACKNOWLEDGMENTS

Thank you, Rosemary Brosnan, for the love you've poured into editing and publishing this novel. Your wisdom, guidance, and belief in this story—and in this writer—made a difference on every page.

Thank you, Meredith Kaffel Simonoff, my agent, champion, and friend, for being the calm in my storm, the lick on my arm, the phosphorus to ignite my potassium chlorate, and whatever else the moment calls for.

Robin Wasserman and Lauren Strasnick read an early draft of this manuscript and offered crucial feedback and support. Thank you, Robin and Lauren, for being friends whom I can trust with the messiest versions of my work and of myself. You understood the best of what this story could be and helped me get it closer.

Thanks to everyone at HarperCollins whose time and talents have gone into the publication of this book, including Courtney Stevenson, Erin Fitzsimmons, Bethany Reis, Ebony LaDelle, Ro Romanello, Jean McGinley, and Kate Jackson.

To my publishing colleagues and friends, and the many incredible writers whose books I had the pleasure of editing: Thank you for the privilege of being part of your professional and creative lives, and for the innumerable ways you've shaped mine. I have learned so much from all of you. Special thanks to David Levithan, Jen Klonsky, Katherine Tegen, Bethany Buck, Craig Walker, Catherine Daly, Mara Anastas, Russell Gordon, Michelle Nagler, Joy Peskin, Beth Dunfey, Kristin Earhart, Donna Bray, and Abby McAden. Hugs to Alex Arnold, Kendra Levin, Tiffany Liao, Michael Strother, Lisa Cheng, Andrew Eliopulos, Caroline Abbey, Emilia Rhodes, Molly O'Neill, Sheila Perkins, Maria Barbo, Sam Margles, Cara Petrus, Zareen Jaffery, Claudia Gabel, Kalah McCaffrey, and Namrata Tripathi. Grateful nods toward Rotem Moscovich, Kristin Ostby, and Alexa Pastor.

This writing life is made so much better by the ever-growing community of writers I am lucky to call friends. Sharing in each other's triumphs, setbacks, and everything in between is such a crucial part of the publishing process—thank you all. Especially fierce hugs go to Terra Elan McVoy, Corey Ann Haydu, Amy Jo Burns, Erin Soderberg Downing, Emily X.R. Pan, Rebecca Serle, Claire Legrand, Christa Desir, Elizabeth Eulberg, Amy Reed, Jessica Martinez, Eileen Cook, Jane Mason, Shaun David Hutchinson, Hannah Moskowitz, Kimberly Sabatini, Micol Ostow, Nora Ericson, Chris Crew, Billy Merrell, Dan Poblocki, Lucas Klauss, Leslie Jamison, and the Electric Eighteens support group. Thank you, Megan McCafferty, Deb Caletti, and Jeff Zentner, for your generous words.

Thanks to all the booksellers, librarians, and educators who help books find their way into the hands and hearts of readers. Thank you, Little Shop of Stories, Labyrinth Books, Community Bookstore, McNally Jackson Books, Princeton Public Library, and Stonington Public Library for shepherding so many books into the hands and heart of *this* reader.

Betts and Jo's friendship is, to me, the heart of this story. I am grateful to the friends, past and present, mentioned and unnamed, who have shaped who I am as a person and writer. Special acknowledgment is owed to Johanna Conterio Geisler, Andrew Garrison, Sulaiman Ijaz, Max Perelman, Abby Ranger (the original cupcake with thorns), Mike McCreless (who first called her that), Jessica Garrison, Rich Hinman, Margaret Meyers, Meg Blocker, Giles Lyon, Rebecca Tuhus-Dubrow, Sophie Danis Oberfield, Sarah Gersick, Katherine Connor Martin, Rachel Pilling, Rebekah Sirois, Sanders Weirs-Haggerty, Joe Metmowlee Garland, Lainie Fefferman, Jascha Narveson, Floor Bear, Owen Lake, Stephanie Su, Ellen Willett, Ellen Lin, Sarah Dodge, April Rourk, and Fatima Petersen.

Much love to my Rissi, Mrose, and Snyder families, especially my parents, Mama and Ati, who have encouraged creative risks in every chapter; my brother, Jeremy, who is in my tallest tales; my husband, Jeff, the best plot twist; our dog, Arugula, who has good ideas; Nono, the best storyteller; and Nini, who knew there would be books.